☠ Pirate McSnottbeard
IN THE
ALIEN SLUG INVASION PANIC

PAUL WHITFIELD

WALKER BOOKS

First published 2018 by Walker Books Ltd
87 Vauxhall Walk, London SE11 5HJ

2 4 6 8 10 9 7 5 3 1

Text and illustrations © 2018 Paul Whitfield

The right of Paul Whitfield to be identified as author and illustrator of this work has been asserted by him in accordance with the Copyright, Designs and Patents Act 1988

This book has been typeset in Stempel Schneidler and LTC Pabst Oldstyle

Printed and bound in Great Britain by CPI Group (UK) Ltd, Croydon, CR0 4YY

British Library Cataloguing in Publication Data:
a catalogue record for this book is
available from the British Library

ISBN 978-1-4063-7309-7

www.walker.co.uk

MIX
Paper from
responsible sources
FSC® C020471

For Milie and Will,
Lorraine and Robyn

A HUMUNGOUS LIE

There's a HUMUNGOUS lie in this book.

See if you can spot it.

I'll give you a hint: it's NOT the next sentence.

Alien slug monsters kidnapped my parents on Wednesday.

I know that seems like a lie, but it would be a dumb one.

It would be dumb for three reasons:

Things Worth Knowing No. 1

by Emilie (me)

1) If you are going to warn people there's a humungous lie in a book, then the thing you don't do is tell the humungous lie straight away.

2) There's no point lying about something like alien slug monsters because no one will believe you.

3) Alien slug monsters kidnap people on Wednesdays.

Perhaps you didn't know that about Wednesdays?

Don't feel bad. I didn't know it either.

But here's the thing: my parents were kidnapped on a Wednesday. And as they're the only people ever to have been snatched by alien slug monsters:

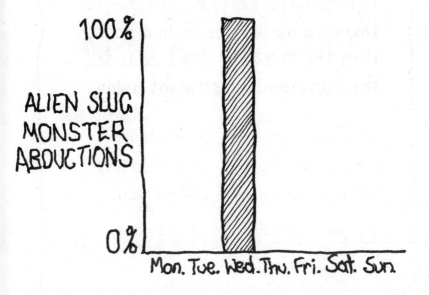

I guess what I am saying is BEWARE OF WEDNESDAYS!

DON'T READ
THIS BOOK

I was asleep when my parents were kidnapped, which isn't that unusual. I was sleeping the last time they were kidnapped too.

It wasn't alien slug monsters that first time. It was **PIRATES** (who really are so awful that they merit capital letters). More precisely, it was the **PIRATE** king *McSnottbeard* – the most awful, most odious, most smelly and second-most hairy **PIRATE** that ever lived!

And before you think you spotted the lie, that's all true. There really was a **PIRATE** *McSnottbeard*.

I say was, because the last time I saw him he'd been struck by lightning, slid off the

side of a tower and
plunged hundreds
and possibly
thousands of
feet into an
angry sea.
You can
read about it
in my last book.
I wouldn't,
though.
It's scary.
Then again it isn't
as scary as this book.
Which is why
you should put this
book down.

Go on.

Close it up and slip it back in the bookcase.
You'll sleep better at night and won't jump at
every unexplained bump in your house.

STILL READING?

Well, I warned you.

And hey, on the bright side, not everything in this book is scary. There's a reasonably nice nine-year-old girl.

That's me: Emilie.

There's also an eleven-year-old boy called
William. He's my brother. I call him Will
and you can too. He isn't scary, but he can be
grumpy. That's him just there.

You can only see the back of his head
because he's at his computer, which is pretty
much where he always is since he got it for his
birthday. Let's not disturb him just yet. He gets
angry if you speak to him when he is playing.
Actually he gets angry if you even say he is
playing.

"I am not playing," he'll growl. "I'm coding."

"Looks like playing," I'll say.

"Only because you know nothing about coding."

That's true. But I'd never admit it. My brother already thinks he knows more about everything than me. Which isn't true.

For example, neither of us knew anything about alien slug monsters.

ALIEN SLUG MONSTERS

Here are five things you should know about alien slug monsters:

Things Worth Knowing No. 2
by Emilie

1) Alien slug monsters are the worst kind of aliens. They are also the worst kind of slugs. And the worst kind of monsters.

2) Scientists haven't found any evidence alien slug monsters exist. Then again they haven't exactly been looking.

3) Alien slug monsters are about as big as basketball players. Which is huge for slugs but average for monsters.

4) Alien slug monsters have massive sharp teeth, but mostly eat plants. Then again man-eating sharks also have massive sharp teeth but mostly eat fish, so "mostly" isn't that comforting when it comes to massive sharp teeth.

5) Alien slug monsters are famous (though not on Earth) for their slime, which comes in two forms: slippery and sticky. Both are awful.

I didn't know any of those things that Wednesday morning, which was unfortunate, as I was soon to discover.

But even worse was the other thing I didn't know: namely that during the night alien slug monsters had oozed into my house, slimed up the stairs, slid into my bedroom to watch me sleep, then slid out again to steal my parents.

I didn't know any of that because, like I said, I was asleep.

A-SALTED

I would have stayed asleep too, but I dreamed that someone with fishy breath was rubbing wet sandpaper on my face.

I woke to find the cat licking me.

"Ummpff," I grumbled as I pushed him away. "Ouch!" I added as something hard bounced off my head. The cat had brought a salt shaker. "Prrrrrrrr," said Eiffel, which is the cat's name.

Then he turned around and began to clean himself.

That was strange.

I don't mean the cleaning. Cats are always doing that. But Eiffel rarely visits me. And he NEVER drops bits of tableware on my head.

I probably should have stopped to think about that, but I was still sleepy and not much in a thinking mood.

"You want to go out?" I mumbled as I picked up the salt shaker, swung my feet out of bed and planted them on the wet floor.

I think we can all agree that a wet floor is strange too. If I hadn't been so sleepy I would definitely have stopped to think about that.

And if I had, I would have saved myself a lot of pain at the start of the next chapter.

But I was very sleepy. So instead of thinking I stood up – briefly.

EMERGENCY PLAN A! B! C! D! ETC!

My feet shot out from underneath me and I hit
the floor with a slap and a squelch.

Or a **SLAPCH**.

"Owwwww," I groaned from the floorboards
and went to rub my head. A glob of green slime

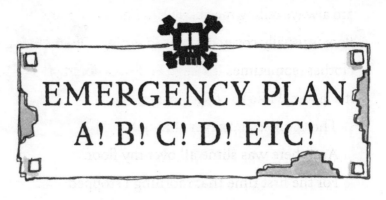

dropped from my hand onto
my cheek.

Now, I don't
know what
kind of kid you
are. Perhaps
you are one
of those tidy
ones my parents

are always telling me about. But I'm not. So my
floor is usually covered with something. Often it's
clothes, sometimes it's Lego and occasionally
it's leaves. I like to collect leaves.

The thing is, it's never slime.

And there was slime all over my floor.

For the first time that morning I stopped
to think. And what I thought was: "Time to
launch Emergency Plan A."

"Mum! Dad!" I shouted.

I waited for the footsteps that would signal
my rescue, but the house was silent.

I moved to Plan B.

"Mum! Dad!" I shouted louder.

You might have noticed Plan B is much like
Plan A. It also happens to be the same as
Plan C, Plan D, Plan E and my other plans all
the way through to Z. I made it to about Plan G
before I gave up and decided to rescue myself.

SLIP AND SLIME

At first I tried wriggling out of my room. It didn't work. After that I tried squirming, then writhing and, finally, just threw myself about.

I made about as much progress as a whale on a motorbike.

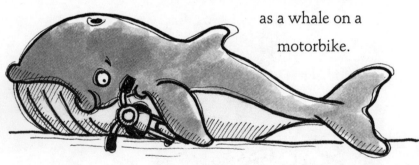

I looked back to see if I could push off from the bed, but I was too far away. From my mattress the cat watched me out of a half-closed eye.

"You could help," I said.

The cat blinked, then yawned. He stood, arched his back, walked to the edge of the mattress, squatted, waggled his bum then launched himself at me.

"Wait!" I screamed. "What are you..."

I screamed all over again as Eiffel landed and dug his claws into my back.

Then I screamed one last time, but with joy, as we slid right out of my door.

BANANAS

My face squeaked on dry floorboards as we came to a stop in the corridor.

I was relieved to be out of my room but still concerned by Mum and Dad's absence. Oh, and I was absolutely terrified by the deep green goop plastered down the hallway to my parents' room.

On the bright side, the few steps between me and my brother's door were slime free.

Here are four things you should know about my brother:

Things Worth Knowing No.3
by Emilie

1) Will was a PIRATE hunter. Really!

2) He also went to wizard school and once made me jump into a volcano.

3) He doesn't do any of those things since Mum and Dad gave him a computer.

4) Now he mostly just sits in front of his screen.

"Will!" I cried as I burst into his room. "There's slime all over…"

I stopped.

Will wasn't in his bed. In his place was a pillow, a book and Mr Bananas, the stuffed monkey he pretends he doesn't sleep with.

"Oh no!" I shouted at the monkey. "They got him!"

To be clear, I didn't expect Mr Bananas to respond.

I also didn't know who I was talking about when I said "they". But I was beginning to suspect there was definitely a "they" and that "they" were responsible for what was turning out to be the worst Wednesday ever.

And that's when I heard the noise.

IT'S BEHIND YOOOOU!

"Click ... click ... clickety, click, click."

Something was in the room.

"Click ... click ... click, click, clack."

AND it was just behind me.

I froze. After everything that had already happened that morning there was no telling what weirdness was behind my back. But, if I had to guess, I would have said it was a giant metal insect walking on tin foil.

"Click ... click ... click, clickety, clickety, click."

And it sounded close.

I grabbed the only weapon within reach. It wasn't ideal – a bit too soft, a bit too cute and way too much like a monkey.

Then I took a deep breath, yelled a battle cry (that may well have been "Please don't hurt me!"), spun and unleashed death by stuffed toy.

BABBLE AND BURN

One thing I forgot to mention about my brother is that he tends to wear headphones while sitting at his computer. That's important, because it explains why he hadn't heard me come into his room – or reacted to my battle cry.

"Click … click … clickety, click, click," he typed in the brief moment before Mr Bananas connected with his head and sent his headphones flying.

"Ooops," I said.

Will turned with a face like a storm (the tropical sort that comes with cyclones, lightning and the risk of injury).

"Three seconds," he growled.

"What?" I said.

"That's how long you have to explain why you hit me with a monkey. After that, I am going to deliver the most blistering Twister Burn in the history of sibling-torture."

RISKYPEDIA
The Adventurer's Encyclopedia

>> TWISTER BURN

A Twister Burn is one of the most painful and satisfying ways to punish a younger sister or brother. It is applied by gripping an arm with both hands then twisting in opposite directions. See also: Things you will definitely get in trouble for.

"Mum and Dad aren't answering," I blurted.

"There better be more." My brother rubbed his palms, blew on them and leaned forward in his chair.

"Slime!" I shouted. "There's slime everywhere, Plan A and Plan B didn't work, I was a whale on a motorbike and Eiffel brought me a salt shaker." The threat of a Twister Burn will make you babble.

"OK," Will said, sitting back and patting the cat, who had jumped onto his desk. "You know that doesn't make any sense?"

I nodded.

"Do you want to start again?"

I nodded.

"Slime?" asked Will.

"All over my room, and down the corridor. It's slippery."

"Salt shaker?"

I held up the container for Will to see.

"Plan A?"

"Shouting for Mum and Dad," I said. "They didn't answer."

"Was that also Plan B?"

I nodded.

"I am not even going to ask about the whale."

"Probably best."

There is a saying that goes: "A problem shared is a problem halved." But when you're a nine-year-old with a brother who likes to refer to himself as "the responsible one", the saying should be: "A problem shared isn't your problem any more."

Either way, I felt better. The slime seemed less worrying, the salt shaker less weird. Everything just seemed a bit more under control and normal.

Until the cat went and ruined it by typing on the computer.

YOU'VE GOT TO BE KITTEN ME!

"Eiffel!" Will shouted.

"Hang on." I grabbed Will's arm as he went to push the cat away. "Look at the screen."

Alien slug monsters stole the people who give me food.

"Did you write that?" I asked.

Will shook his head.

Eiffel stepped on the keyboard, shuffled his feet, then turned a quick circle before flopping down and closing his eyes.

Now the computer read:

```
Alien slug monsters stole the
people who give me food.
You need to save them. I am
getting hungry. Put on socks.
All of them. Don't forget
the salt.
XZXZXZZXXZXZZXZZXXZZZXZZZZZZ
```

My brother and I looked at each other.

"Might be an accident," I suggested.

"It's a very specific accident," said Will. "Particularly the bit about salt."

"What about the Xs and Zs?"

"I think that's just where he fell asleep."

"But that means … oh no!" I ran for the door.

My feet flew out from beneath me for the second time that morning, though this time it was because Will had grabbed my collar.

"Socks," he said. "Eiffel said to put on socks."

Now, I know that wearing socks to battle aliens makes about as much sense as putting on clean underwear to armwrestle a giant. But our cat had just typed on a computer, so sense had evidently packed its bags and gone on holiday.

We put on Will's socks – every last one of them.

"What now?" I asked, surveying my newly massive feet.

"Now we save our parents," said Will, clenching his fists heroically, before ruining it by tripping over his huge feet.

"Be careful," I said as he stumbled into the corridor. "It's slippery."

Will poked his head back through the door. "Get the cat and the salt."

STICKY STUCK IN THE MUCK

If you're expecting this chapter to be full of comedy sliding, you are going to be disappointed. If that's not what you are expecting, then you probably paid attention to point five on that list of things you should know about alien slug monsters. You can go back and check it if you like.

When I entered the corridor I found Will just standing there. "Why aren't you saving our parents?" I asked.

"Stop!" shouted Will. "The slime!"

"Slippery isn't it," I said as I carefully moved over to stand beside him.

"No." Will looked at me in horror. "It's sticky."

I tried to take another step but I couldn't move.

I was stuck to the floor like chewing gum that had been dipped in honey, covered in superglue and then nailed down.

"What bit of 'stop' didn't you understand?" asked Will.

I ignored him. "What now?"

Eiffel meowed in my arms, then looked down at my feet.

"Socks?" I said to myself.

Very slowly I lifted one leg straight up. The outside sock stuck to the ground, but my foot slipped out. I took a step. My foot stuck again but I wriggled the toes on my back foot and it slipped free of the outer sock too.

I took another step.

"Socks!" I shouted triumphantly as I plodded towards Mum and Dad's room.

I bet you can't guess what I found there.

Did you guess? What did you guess?

Did you guess a hippopotamus wearing a bikini and a tea-cup while riding a skateboard?

WRONG!

WHAT I FOUND

What I found was nothing.

Well, not exactly nothing. There was heaps of slime. It was all over the floor, dripping from the ceiling and running out the window.

What I didn't find was my mum and dad.

"They got them!" I cried as Will joined me in the room.

"Who?" asked Will.

I looked at him a little confused. "Our parents!"

Will rolled his eyes. "I meant who are 'they'?"

"Slug monsters," I said, rolling my eyes back at him. My brother and I punctuate most of our conversations with eye rolling.

"And what *is* a slug monster?" Will asked.

RISKYPEDIA
The Adventurer's Encyclopedia

>>ALIEN SLUG MONSTERS
There is absolutely nothing nice to say about alien slug monsters (scientific name Slimax Intergalacticus). And because this encyclopedia believes that if you can't say something nice, you shouldn't say anything at all, that is all it has to say.

I looked to the cat for help. He blinked, meowed happily then jumped from my arms to the bed and lay down.

The truth was that the only thing we knew about alien slug monsters was that they had our parents.

But we were about to learn more.

In THREE seconds.

TWO seconds.

ONE.

Through my parents' open window we heard the whine of jet engines starting.

FILTHY SOCKS AND FLYING SAUCERS

Will and I looked to the window. Then at each other. Then down at our feet. We were down to our last socks.

Remember how I said I am not tidy? Well, if messiness is a disease then I caught it from my dad. In the corner of the room was his usual pile of dirty clothes.

"Dad's socks," said Will.

He took a huge step, planting his foot on a crumpled T-shirt, then picked a handful of sports socks out of the pile and threw them my way.

The smell hit me before the socks did. I held my breath and put them on, then stepped to the window where Will was already looking out at the garden.

"Cripes!" I said.

"Cool," said Will, who appeared to have misjudged the seriousness of the situation.

UP, UP AND AWAY

There were three flying saucers in all. Two were wobbling a few feet in the air as they struggled to lift huge blocks of hardened slime.

The other one was on the ground and in big trouble when Mum found out what it had done to her roses.

I stared at the slime blocks. "Is that...?"

"Mum and Dad," finished Will.

The whine of the engines grew loud enough to rattle my head. My eyes began to shake so violently I feared they would work their way loose. I closed them as a precaution.

Just as I did there was a massive bang and a violent hiss, like a can of drink being opened by a lightning bolt.

And then … nothing.

I opened my eyes. Where the saucers with our parents had been there were now two trails of fire leading up through the clouds.

"Where'd they go?" I whispered to Will.

"Up," he said.

"Mum and Dad…" I left the words hanging, too stunned to finish the sentence.

Will's eyes gleamed with anger, like they do when I hand him an empty packet of sweets I forgot we were meant to share.

"We are going to get them," he said.

"Uh huh." I nodded gently. I was still a little stunned.

"And we are going to do it by getting in that." He pointed at the remaining flying saucer.

My gentle nod turned into a little shake of my head.

"And that means we have to capture that," Will said, moving his arm to point at the biggest garden pest the world has ever seen.

I shook my head a lot.

THINGS I "DISLIKE VERY STRONGLY"

My dad doesn't like slugs. The reason he doesn't like them is exactly the same as the reason I do like them: they eat the beans in his vegetable patch.

I hate beans.

Mum thinks I should say I dislike things rather than hate them. She says that hate is a very strong word. I don't think it is too strong when it comes to beans.

Anyway, because I hate beans, I wasn't terribly upset that there was a seven-foot slug in Dad's vegetable patch. I was even a little happy to see it was eating the beans one whole plant at a time.

But I WAS terribly sorry to *hear* it eating.

Here are five sounds I ~~hate~~ dislike very strongly:

Things I Hate No. 1
by Emilie

1) The buzz of a mosquito at night.

2) The smash of anything I was told not to touch.

3) PIRATES singing.

4) The word "homework".

5) Anyone (or anything) eating with their mouth open.

There shouldn't really be five things on that list.

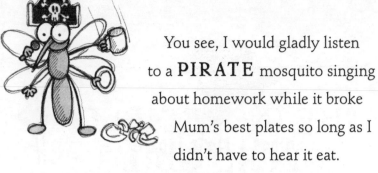

You see, I would gladly listen to a **PIRATE** mosquito singing about homework while it broke Mum's best plates so long as I didn't have to hear it eat.

I really hate (sorry, Mum) the sound of anything eating. And nothing on Earth had ever eaten as loudly as that slug.

"That's DISGUSTING!" I groaned.

I might have groaned too loud.

OK, I definitely groaned too loud.

Down in the garden the slug's eyes swiveled towards Will and me.

It sat up, chewed (too loudly) a few more times, then flopped towards the flying saucer.

Slowly, very slowly, it began to make its get-away.

THE INCREDIBLE GECKO GIRL

"We have to get down there," said Will as he grabbed the duvet off my parents' bed and threw it over the slime-soaked windowsill. He held out more of Dad's dirty socks. "Put these on your hands. And one in your mouth."

"In my mouth?"

"And on your hands."

"But…"

"No time to explain," said Will. "If the slug reaches the ship before we do, Mum and Dad are gone for ever."

I nodded reluctantly as I slipped the salt shaker inside the socks on my hands. Then holding my breath I shoved a sock in my mouth.

It tasted as bad as it smelt.

"What now?" I asked, though with the sock in my mouth it came out as "Gmff".

"Emilie," said Will, suddenly looking caring in a way that made me worried. "We have to do something you won't like."

"No, we don't," I mumbled through the sock.

"It's OK," said Will. "I have a plan."

Will having a plan definitely isn't OK. On a scale of one to ten, ten being a chocolate milkshake and one being a swim with piranhas, Will's plans typically rate about three.

"We are going to climb out the window," said Will, failing to improve his average.

"WE ARE ON THE FIRST FLOOR!" I gmffed.

"The outside of the house is covered in slime."

All of a sudden I understood why I had socks on my hands.

"Our hands and feet will stick," said Will encouragingly. "Just like in that movie, *Gecko Girl*."

I'd never seen *Gecko Girl*. And there was no way I was voluntarily climbing out the window.

Unfortunately for me, it turned out that volunteering wasn't part of Will's plan.

NOT READY, DEFINITELY NOT READY!

My feet swung in the air.

"Ready?" asked Will in that way doctors do when they are holding a needle and don't care how ready you are. I clung to his hand. "Just touch the slime," he said.

I looked at the thin layer of goo on the wall and tried to say no.

Will's hand slipped. "Quick!" he shouted.

I shoved my hands against the wall, screamed through the sock in my mouth and prepared to fall to my death.

Only I didn't die. Or even fall.

I stuck to the wall.

I looked up at Will in amazement.

"Good plan, isn't it?" He grinned as he clambered out the window with the cat clinging to his shoulders.

"Gmff," I said with relief.

Carefully – very, very carefully – I climbed down, leaving a trail of socks as I went.

At the bottom I pulled the sock out of my mouth and retrieved the salt shaker before shedding my remaining socks.

"What do I do with these?" I asked Will as I tried to scrape the taste of Dad's feet from my tongue.

"Keep the salt," said Will. "The cat clearly thinks it's important. You can chuck the sock."

I chucked it at Will.

It slapped moistly onto his face.

"Hey!" he yelled.

"You made me put that sock in my mouth just to keep me quiet!"

"Why did you throw it at me?" Will said in an unjustifiably injured tone.

"Why was it in my mouth?"

"Why'd you throw it at me?"

Here are four annoying things my brother does with annoying regularity:

Things Worth Knowing No. 4
<u>by Emilie</u>

1) Answers my questions with a question.

2) Rolls his eyes.

3) Eats all his beans (possibly because he likes them but probably just to make me look bad).

4) Never lets me have the last word.

We might have kept on arguing but the cat
bit my ankle. "Ouch," I yelped. "Don't tell me
you're on his side?"

Eiffel rolled his eyes (I didn't even know cats
could do that) then turned and trotted towards
the alien slug monster – which, to judge by
its slime trail, had made about three inches of
progress towards getting away.

I looked sheepishly at Will – having a cat
point out that you are being silly is a little
uncomfortable. Will shrugged. Then we ran
after the cat.

THIS IS NOT
TRUE!
WILL

NOT MUCH OF A PLAN

"Will," I said as we ran. "Do you have a plan for the slug?"

"Nope," puffed Will (whose fitness had really gone downhill since the computer arrived). "I'm hoping it'll come to me when we need it."

We skidded to a halt a metre away from the slug. Our garden isn't very big.

"OK," I said. "We need it."

"Right," said Will. "Ummm … got it."

Will turned to the slug, took a step forward, put his hands out and shouted, "Stop!"

In truth, the alien was moving so slowly it was hard to be sure it had even started. I looked at Will in disbelief. "That's your plan?"

"I'd be happy to hear your alternative."

I thought for a second. "Stop!" I shouted at the slug.

The alien didn't even look at us.

"OK. I have another plan," said Will.

"Great."

"You grab it by the tail then—"

"Woah!" I interrupted. "No!"

"Think of Mum and Dad," said Will.

"OK." I nodded. "I'll think of them. You grab it."

Will huffed then slowly reached out a hand and poked the slug with his finger.

"That's not grabbing," I said.

"I'm working up to it."

My brother took a deep breath and then, to my horror and considerable admiration, wrapped both arms around the slug's slimy tail.

"That is our spaceship," he grunted as he pulled. "We need it."

SLUGGING IT OUT

An enormous wet roar tore out of the slug's mouth, and we learned one more thing about alien slug monsters: they may not be quick in a straight line, but they are as fast as lightning on the spot.

The slug whipped around to face my brother. Its huge jaws opened to reveal teeth as big as skateboards.

Will tumbled backwards.

"I think you annoyed it," I said unnecessarily.

The monster swayed briefly then lunged at my brother, who scrambled away just in time to leave its teeth snapping on air.

"Definitely annoyed it," I said.

The slug reared, moved from side to side like

a cobra and struck
again. Teeth crunched
inches from Will's
face, and snapped
again as he rolled.

He might even have
rolled all the way to
safety if he hadn't got
stuck under the flying
saucer.

The slug growled.
The muscles in its neck
rippled as its jaws opened
wider. It prepared to
strike.

IF I'D HAD MORE TIME

I didn't really stop to think about what I did next. To be honest, if I'd had more time, and perhaps a pencil and paper to make a list, I might have done something different.

FOR and AGAINST: Jumping Between Will and a Murderous Space Slug
by Emilie

FOR	AGAINST
Prove I'm brave	Probably die
Save my brother's life	Probably die
Distract alien so Will can get in the saucer and save our parents	Probably die
Win my brother's lasting gratitude	**Be dead**

Sure, the "against" column lacks variety but you have to admit it's compelling.

"Stop it!" I shouted as I jumped between Will and the slug. "Someone is going to get hurt," I added, mainly because that's what Mum would have said. Will looked up at me with a mixture of worry and relief. The slug looked down at me with a mixture of slime and absolute terror.

That's not a mistake. The slug really was afraid of me. Or, at least, my hand. And not so much my hand either, but the salt shaker that I had mostly forgotten I was holding.

FIRST CONTACT

RISKYPEDIA
The Adventurer's Encyclopedia

>> SALT
Salt (or sodium chloride) is a common mineral and a delicious seasoning used in many savoury dishes. It is also lethal to slugs and snails, and does very little to improve their taste.

I lifted the salt. The slug's eyes followed my hand. I lowered it and down went the eyes. Then I jiggled the shaker, spilling some salt on the grass next to me.

The slug squealed.

"Are you afraid of this?" I held up the shaker.

The slug nodded.

"What!?" I shouted, causing the alien to shrink away in fright. "You understand me?"

The slug nodded again.

"Did you see that?" I turned to my brother. "It understands!"

"That's nice," said Will as he picked himself up from the ground. "Ask it if it is going to try to eat me again."

The slug shook its head.

"It says no," I huffed. "It understands you too." I was a little disappointed to discover my gift of alien communication wasn't unique.

"Good," said Will as he took the salt from me. "You," my brother pointed the salt shaker at the slug, "will take me and my sister—"

Behind Will, the cat miawoed.

"And the cat," added Will, eyeing the cat suspiciously.

"You will take us all on that

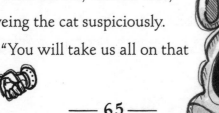

flying saucer and help us save our parents."

The slug's eyes opened wide and it shook its head. My eyes opened wide too. It hadn't really sunk in that we would actually be getting on the spaceship.

"And you will do it quickly or I will season you to within an inch of your life," said Will.

The slug let out a bubbly squeal and shrunk so far back into itself that it was in danger of turning inside out.

"Stop that," I said, snatching the salt out of Will's hand. "You're scaring him … or her … or … it."

Will harrumphed and climbed into the spaceship. "Get the cat," he said grumpily, pointing to where Eiffel lay in the grass with his eyes closed.

Cats really can fall asleep anywhere.

I put the salt down, picked up the cat and, very reluctantly, followed my brother and the alien slug monster onto the flying saucer.

BIG OUT THERE

Space is big.

Bigger than you think.
Or at least bigger
than I thought,
which is what I
was thinking as the
earth shrunk behind our
flying saucer.

"There's so much room," I said.

"Not in here," said Will.

That was true. The thing about the
flying saucer was that it was built for one.
On the upside, the one it was built
for was an enormous slug, so it
was quite large.

— 67 —

On the downside, the flying saucer was mostly full of enormous slug.

Will and I were squished up against the window to avoid touching the alien. As a result, we didn't have much choice but to stare out at our disappearing planet.

"I hope we see it again," Will said.

I shivered. "We shouldn't be here."

"What do you mean?" asked Will.

"We are just kids."

"So?"

"So, kids don't leave their planets in flying saucers."

"They do now," said Will.

We watched the earth until it was just another dot of light among millions of others.

"Where are we going?" I asked.

"Don't know."

I stared out into space for a bit.

"Do you think we're nearly there?"

WHAT THE CAT KNEW

We weren't nearly there.

In fact, we weren't even remotely nearly there.

"We are … two and a bit light-years away," said Will, as he looked at a corner of the spaceship's control panel that looked very much like the sat-nav in our car.

TIME TO ARRIVAL: 764,323 YEARS

DESTINATION: MOTHER SHIP

+

−

SPEED

1,756 MPH

DISTANCE

2 LIGHT-YEARS

i-mlost

"That's not much," I said.

Will looked over at me. "You don't know what a light-year is, do you?

"No" I said. "But I know what two is, and it isn't a lot."

RISKYPEDIA
The Adventurer's Encyclopedia

>> LIGHT-YEAR

Space is huge. So huge that things in it tend to be too far apart for humans to comprehend in terms of miles. Scientists solved this problem by coming up with light-years, a measure of distance so big that no one can comprehend it either.

It turns out two light-years is about eleven trillion, seven hundred and fifty-seven billion, two hundred and fifty-one million, eighty-two thousand, four hundred and ninety-six miles ... and a thousand or so metres.

The trip was going to take ages.

But then again, time is relative.

I don't really understand what that means.
But it's the reason we arrived so quickly
despite being so far away. Or at least that was
how the cat explained it, only I wasn't really
concentrating on the explanation because

THE

CAT

WAS

SPEAKING!

EMILIE DOOLITTLE

Much like my understanding of relative time, my understanding of why I was able to talk to the cat is a little sketchy. But I know how it happened.

While Will and I were squashed up against the window avoiding the slug, the cat was stretched out on the ship's control panel. He was meowing at the slug monster, which was kind of bubbling back at the cat.

"I think they're talking," I said to Will.

"It'd be nice to know what they are saying," he said.

The cat and the slug both turned to us. Then Eiffel reached out a paw and started to type.

"You need to lick me," read the message on a screen above the control panel.

I chuckled. "Would a scratch do?"

Eiffel tapped some more.

"You need to swallow a fur ball so you can understand."

"I think he's serious," said Will.

I shook my head. "Well, I am seriously not licking the cat."

"Chemicals in my fur will supercharge your brain's language ability," typed the cat.

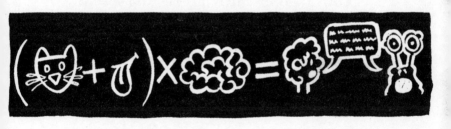

Will nodded.

I looked at my brother. "Why are you nodding?"

"He seems to know what he is talking about."

"He's a cat!" I said. "He doesn't even know what day it is!"

"It's Wednesday," typed Eiffel. "And in about a minute, on this Wednesday, we are going to warp to faster than light speed. Moments later we'll arrive at the mother ship where you'll have to explain to thousands of very bad-tempered slugs why you kidnapped their friend and hijacked their flying saucer, and convince them to give your parents back. YOU NEED TO UNDERSTAND THEM!"

"OK," I said. "Perhaps he does know what day it is."

NEVER LAUGH AT A SPACE SLUG

Here are four things you should earnestly hope you never have to do:

Things Worth Knowing No. 5
by Emilie

1) Eat beans.

2) Hug a giant slug.

3) Dance with Damien "Sticky" Kanicky from my school.

4) Lick a cat.

I leant over the cat, stuck out my tongue and licked. Then, more reluctantly than I have perhaps ever done anything in my whole life, I swallowed.

Nothing happened.

"It doesn't work," I said to Will, though not until he had licked the cat too.

"What bit of it didn't work?" said Eiffel.

My jaw dropped and I squealed with delight. "I understand the cat!"

Eiffel sighed. "This trip is going to be quick, relatively speaking. Maybe you could use it to practise being quiet?"

I clapped my hands with excitement. "Say something else!"

"Quiet, pathetic human," growled the slug. "I need silence to calculate the jump to warp speed."

I squealed again. "I understand the slug too!"

The giant alien turned towards me and leant forward until its huge mouth was only inches away. Its breath smelt like beans. "I am not 'the slug'," said the slug. "My name is Fairy-Petal Wigglybum."

I looked at the huge mass of slime, muscle and razor-sharp teeth in front of me. "Are you sure?" I asked.

"Yes," said the slug. "Why?"

"It's just, Fairy-Petal is quite a delicate name and you…" I stopped as I reconsidered the wisdom of insulting a space monster.

"Wigglybum?" sniggered Will, who clearly wasn't worried about that.

The slug rose up to its full height and puffed out its chest. "The Wigglybums are feared warriors," it said. "Many a planet has trembled before a Wigglybum."

Will burst out laughing, which made me giggle.

The slug growled.

"I wouldn't do that if I was you," said Eiffel.

"What?" asked Will.

"Laugh at an alien slug monster."

"Why not?"

The cat shrugged. "Because they have very long teeth, very short tempers and absolutely no sense of humour."

Will and I stopped giggling.

The slug eyed us a little longer then turned back to the control panel. "Use those disgusting appendages to hold on," it said.

"You mean our arms?" I asked. "Why?"

"Because, you horrid, hairy homo sapien, we are about to jump to warp speed, and I don't want you bouncing around leaking blood."

I looked for something to hold on to, but everything was smooth glass, polished metal or slimy slug. So I held onto the only other available thing.

And reassuringly, Will held on to me too.

TEN ... NINE ... WAIT!

> ## RISKYPEDIA
> ## The Adventurer's Encyclopedia
>
> ### >> WARP SPEED TRAVEL
> Travelling at warp speed overcomes the
> painful reality that flying millions
> of miles in space is time-consuming
> and boring. It does this by squashing
> space to make distances shorter. Humans
> haven't yet discovered warp speed
> travel. Then again the list of things
> humans haven't yet discovered is so
> long you'd need to travel at warp
> speed to get to the end of it.

The inside of the spaceship began to flash a
worrying shade of red.

"What's that light?" I asked. "Is it bad?"

"Red lights are rarely good," said Will.

"Warp drive engaging," said a metallic voice.

"No ... wait," I yelled.

The cat leapt into a gap between the control panel and the floor, shaking with fear.

"There should be a countdown," I pleaded.

"Warping in three, two..." said the metallic voice.

"From ten!" I yelled. "You're meant to start from ... aaaaargh!"

The flying saucer lurched forward.

I immediately lost my grip on Will and crashed against the back window. Then I shot up into the roof as the flying saucer plunged.

"Aaaaargh!" I yelled from the top of the saucer's glass dome.

"Ooooh," I added as I watched the stars rush past, in a display so dazzling I forgot to be scared.

Then the ship stopped and I remembered about being scared all over again. I closed my eyes and screamed as I plummeted to the hard floor.

NOT THE FLOOR

The floor turned out to be far softer and quite a bit squishier than I had imagined.

"Release me," said the slug.

I let go and slumped onto the actual floor. Next to me the cat was still shaking with fright.

The ship's voice crackled. "Warping complete. Thank you for flying with Sluggish Airways. Please be careful when opening overhead compartments as luggage may have moved during the flight."

The cat began to shake even more violently.

"It's OK," I said. "I think we've arrived."

"That's what I'm afraid of," said Eiffel.

I tried to imagine what could be worse than warp speed travel. Nothing came to mind.

It turned out that was only because I wasn't looking out the window.

But Will was.

"WOW!"

he said.

THE MOTHER OF ALL SHIPS

"Wow," I said as I lifted myself off the floor and stood next to Will.

In front of us was a spaceship as big as a small country.

"S.S. Mum," said Will, reading the side of the ship.

"The mother ship," said Eiffel, retreating further into his hiding place.

"Sounds friendly," I said.

"It isn't."

"How do you know?"

The cat stuck his head out.

"Because the only thing in the whole galaxy meaner than one alien slug monster is two alien slug monsters," he said. "And the only thing meaner than two is three and ... well, that ship contains ALL the alien slug monsters."

"All of them?" I asked.

"Hundreds of thousands," said the cat.

WHAT THE CAT KNEW 2

As we approached the massive ship it became clear that massive wasn't nearly big enough to describe it. Super-duper-mega-enormous was closer, but still too small. Nonetheless, I was still struggling with the idea that an entire species lived on just one spaceship.

"Don't they have a planet?" I asked Eiffel.

"They did," said Eiffel. "A beautiful, green planet that was full of just the kinds of plants slugs love to eat. And that's what they did:

they ate and they ate and then they ate some more. Until one day they stopped."

"Were they full?" I asked.

"They'd eaten everything," said the cat.

"So, why didn't they starve?" asked Will.

Eiffel sighed. "During all that time eating they stumbled upon intergalactic space flight. It took them one hundred and fifty-seven years to pack their civilisation onto the mother ship."

"Doesn't seem that long considering they have no arms," I said.

The cat ignored me. "Once everyone was on-board they blasted off and travelled to another beautiful planet. It took them five hundred and twelve years to unpack – mostly because they hadn't labelled the boxes properly. In fact it took them so long that by the time they'd finished unpacking they had to move again."

"Why?"

"They'd eaten that planet too," said Eiffel. "After that they never bothered to settle down again. Now they just cruise the galaxy eating whatever they stumble across."

"How do you know all that?" I asked.

"Every cat knows that story," said Eiffel. "The first planet the slugs moved to was our planet."

"Oh. I'm sorry," I said, because what else can you say when you find out that your cat is an interplanetary refugee.

"Not half as sorry as you are going to be," said Eiffel.

"Why?"

"Because the slugs are heading for Earth next."

ALIEN ALOHA

Will and I were, obviously, going to have to save
our planet – or at least ask someone else to.

But that'd have to wait.

You see, while the cat had been giving us a
history lesson, our saucer had been flying
at speeds just under terrifying towards the
mother ship. In fact, we'd been going so
fast, that we'd arrived.

"Preparing to dock," said the ship's voice as
we swooped through doors the size of football

pitches into a hangar as big as a city.

The flying saucer stopped, hung in the air for a moment, then plummeted, stopping inches above the floor. I would have screamed, but I had to wait for my stomach to catch up.

Fairy-Petal grinned. "Now you will learn the might of my species."

"Oh dear," said Eiffel as he retreated back under the control panel. I was beginning to doubt the cat would be much help.

The door of our flying saucer hissed open.

Outside was the universe's biggest garage. Tens of thousands of spacecraft stretched out as far the eye could see.

"Will," I said. "How are we going to find Mum and Dad?"

My brother pointed out into the hangar. "We'll get them to show us."

In the distance three slugs were approaching on floating platforms.

Will gave my arm a squeeze. "Don't worry,"

he whispered. "I know exactly what to do."

"How?"

"Saw it in *Galaxy Greetings 2: Alien Aloha.*"

Will stepped out, smiled at the approaching slugs and shouted, "Surprise!"

The slugs didn't look surprised. They looked angry.

THAT EXACT MOMENT

Anyone who has ever seen a science-fiction film knows that first contact with aliens should be made by someone with a uniform and an army, or, at the very least, a leather jacket and big muscles.

We had none of those things, so it was a mystery why Will seemed so happy to see the alien slug monsters.

What I didn't realize was that at this moment he thought we had a secret weapon. If you wait two pages, you can see the exact moment he realizes his mistake.

"Helloooo alien slugs," said Will, waving as the monsters arrived at our spaceship.

"Take me to your leader."

"Earthling invaders," boomed one of the slugs. "I am Kitten-Cuddles JiggleBelly."

"Seriously?" said Will, stifling a giggle.

Behind me Fairy-Petal growled.

"You are trespassing," said Kitten-Cuddles.

Will made a big show of looking around. "I guess we are."

"You are also thieves and kidnappers and will be punished."

My brother nodded enthusiastically, then turned and winked at me.

The slugs looked confused. Polite agreement evidently wasn't what they were expecting. It wasn't what I was expecting either.

"Do you understand what we are saying?" asked Kitten-Cuddles. "Do you need a cat to lick?"

"Oh, no thanks," said Will. "We brought our own."

"Do you want to run away?" asked one of the other slugs.

"Nope," said Will.

"Are you sure?" said Kitten-Cuddles. He sounded a little disappointed.

Will nodded, then leaned in close to me and whispered, "Pass me the salt."

"Sorry?" I said.

"The salt. Slip it into my hand."

"The salt?"

"They'll do whatever we say once they see it."

"I don't have it."

"Well go and get it," said my brother. Then smiling back towards the slugs he chuckled, "Be right with you."

"I put it down," I said.

"OK," said Will. "Pick it up again."

"On Earth."

"What?"

"In our garden," I said. "You told me to get the cat. I needed both hands."

And that, right there, was the exact moment he realized his mistake.

—— 96 ——

RUN!

While Will was coming to terms with the reality of facing thousands of vicious aliens without the help of food seasoning, the slugs were getting impatient.

"You will come now," commanded Kitten-Cuddles.

Will stood motionless, his mouth gaping.

"Just one second," I said to the slugs as I tugged on my brother's sleeve. "Snap out of it. We have to do something."

Will shook his head. "I am out of plans."

I looked at the slugs. Then back at my brother. Then back at the slugs. "Well, I'm not," I said and yanked Will forward. "RUN!"

"Every animal for themselves!" shouted
Eiffel as he shot past us and disappeared
between the parked spacecraft.

"They are running!" cheered Kitten-Cuddles.

"Hurrah!" yelled another slug. "Slime them!"

HOW I GOT CAUGHT

Will and I jumped from the flying saucer just as two gobs of slug-goop splattered where we'd been standing. I dragged my brother with me as I dived between two flying saucers.

"Stay low," said Will from behind me.

"Good thinking," I said, relieved that my brother seemed to have rediscovered his senses. "And we should stick together," I added as I looked over my shoulder.

Will wasn't there.

"Will," I whispered in that way people do when they are actually kind of shouting. There was no reply. "Great," I grumbled and crawled around the side of a saucer to peek out.

Will was nowhere to be seen. Fortunately, neither were the slugs. The hangar seemed empty.

I carefully edged forwards and peered over the top of another saucer.

Right in front of me was the hideous moist face of a giant slug. Its mouth opened into an awful toothy grin.

"BOO!" yelled the monster.

I jumped back between the flying saucers as a wad of slime exploded next to me.

I turned and ran. I ran like my life depended on it (because it did). I wasn't worried about where I was going. I just put my head down, pumped my arms and sprinted.

Which was how I ran into a flying saucer and knocked myself out.

PRISONERS

I woke to find Will staring down at me.

"It's good to see you," he said.

"Is it?"

I was confused, and not just because Will is rarely happy to see me. It turns out confusion is a side effect of hitting your head on a flying saucer.

"Of course," said Will. "Now we can escape from this prison."

I looked around. We were in a small room with shelves stacked full of cleaning supplies. In the corner was a tap with a bucket and mop under it.

"It looks more like a store cupboard than a prison," I said.

"Well, the door's locked," said Will. "So that makes us prisoners."

"Are you sure we aren't cleaners?"
I asked.

Will held up his hands. They were handcuffed. I looked down and saw mine were too.

"Oh," I said. "Where's the cat?"

"He got away," said Will. "I heard the slugs talking about it while you slept."

"I wasn't sleeping. I ran into a flying saucer."

"You what!?"

I changed the subject. "How did you get caught?"

"I didn't. I surrendered."

"You what!?"

Will nodded. "They said if I surrendered I could have dinner with the queen. They call her Mother. That's why it's called the mother ship."

My stomach grumbled, reminding me that I had missed out on breakfast. "Dinner sounds nice," I said. "Why are we trying to escape?"

"Because we're dessert."

BUBBLES

Learning that you are going to be eaten will
ruin your appetite.

"I don't want to be a slug's pudding," I
groaned.

"What?" said Will. "Oh no. The slugs aren't
going to eat us."

I smiled, happy to have misunderstood.

"Something called a fire lizard is going to do
that."

I groaned all over again.

"We need soap," said Will.

I sniffed my armpit. He was right.

"To get the handcuffs off," said Will.

"Oh, right." I nodded. "Couldn't you just
magic them off?"

That's not as silly as it sounds. My brother is a wizard – or at least he was training to be one before his computer came along.

Will shook his head. "There's no magic in space. I can't even do a card trick."

That was both a blow and a relief given all the card tricks I'd had to sit through. "How's soap going to help us?" I asked.

"Not us," said Will. "My cuffs are too tight. But yours will slide right off if we make them slippery."

I jiggled my hands. Will was right, my cuffs were loose.

"OK," I said. "Where do we find soap?"

Will pointed at a container high up on the top shelf and smiled. "There!"

BUBBLE BOTHER

Before things go wrong there's usually a moment when everything seems all right. People call it "the calm before the storm".

That's this bit.

Will opened the bottle of washing-up liquid and gave it a squeeze. Bubbles rose slowly out and floated onto his nose. "Cool," he said, gently blowing a bubble towards his eye, where it popped.

And with that, the storm arrived.

"Arrrrrgh!" screamed Will, clamping a hand over his face – the same hand that was holding the Soapernova. The bottle bounced off his head, sprayed soap into

his other eye then tumbled to the ground and
emptied most of its contents.

"Arrrrrgh!" Will screamed again.

"What should I do?" I yelled.

"Water!" howled Will.

In the corner of the room, the tap dripped
lazily into the bucket.

"Got it," I said and skated over
the soapy floor like a new-
born giraffe on an
ice rink.

I slid to a stop next to the bucket and
grimaced. The water inside was green and
smelled like cheese.

"Quick," whimpered Will.

"But the water—" I started.

"QUICK!"

I shrugged, picked up the bucket and threw the worryingly thick contents at Will. It landed with a thud and slid down his face, forming green bubbles as it mixed with the soap.

"Arrrgggh!" Will shouted. "That's worse and it smells like mature cheddar!"

"I tried to tell you."

"Clean water!"

I wrenched on the tap handle. Water gushed into the bucket, slopping over the sides onto the soapy floor.

A carpet of bubbles began to grow. It was already up to my waist as I pushed my way back to Will. I say pushed, because the bubbles were strangely solid. And they were multiplying. By the time I got to Will I could barely see over the suds.

I reached up and tipped the bucket onto his head.

Water poured down, creating a new explosion of bubbles. Will stood for a second then let out another anguished cry. "I'm blind!" he yelled.

I rolled my eyes. "Take the bucket off."

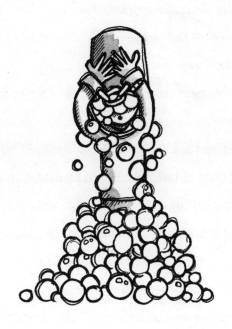

HEAVY CLEANING

"Emilie?" said my brother as he lifted the bucket. "Where are you?"

The bubbles were now over my head.

"Here," I shouted, putting a hand up, which was a pleasant surprise. The handcuffs had slipped off my wrists. "I'm free!"

My brother grunted as he pulled me through the foam.

"Will," I said. "Why are the bubbles heavy?"

Will bent down, fished around on the ground and came up with the bottle of washing-up liquid. He turned it over to read the label on the back.

"Heavy cleaning," said Will.

"Keep out of reach of children," I added.

SOAPERNOVA DEATH BUBBLES

For all your <u>HEAVY</u> cleaning.

Don't mix with water!

KEEP OUT OF REACH OF CHILDREN.

Will dropped the bottle into his pyjama pocket. "We have to get out of here," he said and pushed his way through the bubbles to the door. "We are going to be crushed."

FATAL FOAM

The foam grew and thickened until it was impossible to see anything. It was also nearly impossible to move. Suds weighed on my shoulders and trapped my feet. I tripped and crawled to the door.

"It won't open," said Will.

"What?"

I heard Will rattle the handle.

"Of course it won't open," I groaned from next to his feet. "We are prisoners."

"We have to break it," Will grunted under the growing weight of the bubbles. "Either it breaks or we do."

I pulled myself up Will's leg and together we pushed against the door. Or, at least, that was the theory. In truth, the bubbles were pressing us so hard it was difficult to tell if we were pushing or being crushed.

"It's not moving," I whimpered as I fell back to the ground under the weight of the bubbles. Will grimaced as he gave the door one last shove then slumped somewhere close to me.

"It's no use," he panted through the cloud of suds. "It won't budge."

And then it did.

The lock clicked and the door burst open. Will and I tumbled into the corridor along with tonnes, actual tonnes, of bubbles.

Above us stood a robot.

Or more correctly, what appeared to have once been quite a few different robots, and perhaps some cooking utensils.

"Hello," I said.

The robot's one good eye lit up and there was a faint buzzing sound. A roll of paper emerged from its mouth and fell to the ground.

Will picked it up.

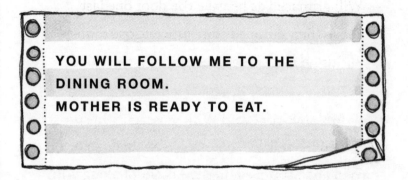

YOU WILL FOLLOW ME TO THE DINING ROOM.
MOTHER IS READY TO EAT.

"Perfect timing," said Will. "We just finished washing up."

E-GOR

We followed the strange little robot down a gleaming white corridor.

"What is that?" I whispered to Will.

"It's an E-gor," said Will, massaging his wrists where the robot had removed his handcuffs.

"Cool," I said. "What's an E-gor?"

"They were in that movie, *Space Junk 3: Low Orbit Litter.*"

I hadn't seen it.

A LONG WALK AND A BRIEF CHAT

Here are four things you should know about E-gors:

Things Worth Knowing No. 6
by Emilie

1) E-gors are heaps of junk. They are made from scrap and upgrade themselves over time using bits that fall off other robots.

2) Their dedication to self-improvement makes them the most reliable robots in the universe.

3) For that reason they are considered indispensable by the universe's most despicable space monsters.

4) Which is why it's never a good thing to meet an E-gor.

The E-gor led us down gleaming white corridors, through dozens of identical sliding doors and past banks of computers. As we walked I began to think.

"Will," I said eventually. "This rescue isn't going well is it?"

"Not so far," said Will.

"In all those movies you watch, is it ever two kids who defeat the evil aliens and save the world?"

"No. It's usually an ace space explorer, or a gang of unlikely rogues."

I thought for a bit. "We are unlikely."

"I think gangs have more than two people," said Will.

We walked on through more white corridors and more sliding doors.

"Will," I said. "Why'd the slugs take our parents?"

Will got the look he gets when he is thinking (which happens to be the same look he gets when he needs to wee).

"Do you need the toilet?" I asked.

"I am thinking," said Will.

We walked on some more.

"Will?"

"Shush."

"But—"

"I'm still thinking," said Will.

"Pffft," I huffed and took matters into my own hands.

EXCUSE ME

I reached forward and tapped the E-gor. The little robot's head spun 180 degrees to face backwards, while its body continued to roll steadily forwards.

"I was wondering," I said as I hurried to keep up, "why did the slugs kidnap our parents?"

The E-gor's eye lit up, there was a brief hum and then a short stub of paper appeared:

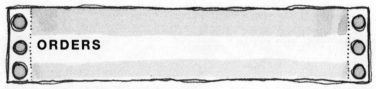

ORDERS

"From Mother?" I asked.

The E-gor's head shook and another piece of paper emerged:

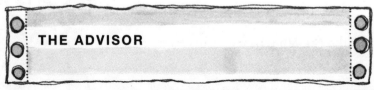

THE ADVISOR

"What's the ADVISOR?"

The E-gor shuddered. There was another buzz and another piece of paper:

ERROR 101: LOW INK

"What? No ... hang on!"

The robot's head turned around and it trundled on even faster. I had to jog just to keep up, which is why I didn't notice the unusually massive set of sliding doors until the E-gor stopped in front of them.

The robot spun and buzzed again and another piece of paper appeared:

**THE
DINING
ROOM!**

"I thought you were out of ink!" I said.

Then the doors opened, and ink suddenly felt like the least of my problems.

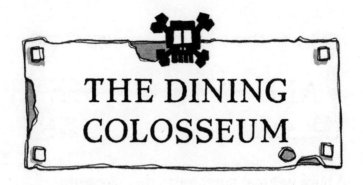

THE DINING COLOSSEUM

I stepped out into a vast circular room with a dirt floor and high stone walls.

"A colosseum," said my brother with a little too much astonishment for my comfort.

"Is that good?"

Will shook his head. "It's where gladiators fight," he said. "And die."

"Then it's lucky we aren't gladiators," I said.

From somewhere in the room a loudspeaker crackled into life. "WELCOME EARTHLING GLADIATORS!"

ALL EYES ON ME

A huge wet roar rang around the colosseum.

It was a terrifying noise. Though not half as terrifying as what was making it.

Above the colosseum's walls, on all sides of the room, rows of seats stretched skywards. Sitting in every single seat was a slug – tens of thousands of them. And every last one was watching us.

MOTHER

"What do we do?" I asked Will.

"I guess we eat," he said, pointing to a table in the centre of the arena.

At the table were two giant slug monsters, who, to my surprise, I recognized. Fairy-Petal and Kitten-Cuddles were seated either side of a stunning golden throne that was positioned in front of some massive red curtains. On our side of the table were two cheap-looking plastic stools.

Will walked confidently towards the table. I shuffled self-consciously after him.

We were almost at our seats before I noticed the throne wasn't empty. On it was a snail, and not a very big one.

In fact it was a completely normal snail-sized snail and would have been unremarkable if it wasn't:

A) Sitting on a throne

B) Wearing a crown

C) Exquisitely well-spoken.

"Dear children," came a voice so serene, regal and beautiful that it made me want to curtsey. "How delightful to meet you. I am Mother, and you, darling things, must be exhausted after your trip. Please sit."

I looked at the tiny gastropod.

"Mother is a snail?" I asked Will.

My brother shrugged. "Makes as much sense as any of this."

Fairy-Petal, who had been watching Mother while she spoke, turned to us and roared, "Mother says you heinous humanoids should sit and do it quickly before I bite your heads off and jettison your bodies into space."

"That is not what she said," I complained.

"Sit," rumbled Fairy-Petal, licking its lips.

I quickly sat on a stool. Will lowered himself slowly. And as he did, he sniffed the air.

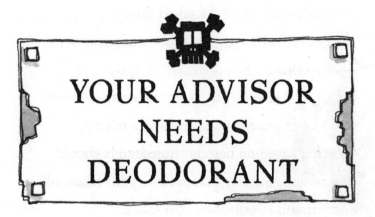

YOUR ADVISOR NEEDS DEODORANT

My parents are always telling me not to do things just because someone else does them. But there are some things that you can't help copying. Yawning and eating crisps are two examples. Sniffing is, unfortunately, another.

So when Will sniffed the air, I sniffed too. I immediately regretted it. The arena stunk of compost, dead fish, old trainers and dirty cat tray.

That's probably how you'd imagine alien slug monsters smelled if you'd ever imagined alien slug monsters existed. But there was something else in that pong. There was a memory I couldn't quite put my finger on – possibly because I had my fingers up my nose to block the smell.

There was a polite cough from the other side of the table. I sheepishly lowered my hands.

"I do so hope that you are hungry," said Mother. "My chefs are the universe's best."

My stomach rumbled.

"Mother said you'll eat what you get and eat it all, if you want to keep your limbs," roared Kitten-Cuddles.

I looked at the giant slug in disbelief. "Worst translators ever," I grumbled.

"Shhh," said Will. "Can you see that?"

I was about to point out that shushing wouldn't help me see, when I noticed what Will was looking at. Behind the throne, in the dark shadows of the red curtains, moved an even darker shadow.

"The ADVISOR?" I asked.

"Hmmf," my brother grunted in that way he does when he isn't really listening.

SPACE SNAKES
AND MOON FROGS

"Shall we eat?" lilted Mother.

A small hatch opened in the wall of the arena and five covered plates, each trailing steam, flew like fighter jets towards the table. They swooped in tight formation before separating and landing gently, one in front of each dinner guest.

"I hope it's chicken," I said. I really like chicken.

"It'll be boiled moon-frogs or fried space-snakes," said Will.

"How do you know?"

"*Cosmic Cooks II: Nebular Nibbles.*"

I screwed up my face.

"What does space snake taste like?"

"Chicken," said Will.

There was a blare of trumpets from the loudspeaker. The covers on the plates rose and steam flooded out so for a brief moment I couldn't see what was there.

But I could smell it.

My heart sunk.

"Beans," said Will happily.

For the first time since my parents were kidnapped I felt like crying.

CANDY FLOSS

There's lots of things I don't like to eat. Dad says it's because I am fussy. I say it's because I have refined taste.

"That's just another way of saying fussy," says Dad.

"Yeah, a refined way," I say.

Anyway, I am not fussy. There are heaps of things I absolutely love to eat. I even stuck a list of them to the fridge to help my parents with the shopping.

Apparently, my parents can't read.

Emilie's Grocery List
1) Candy floss
2) Marshmallows
3) Jelly Babies
4) Bubble gum
5) NOT BEANS

THERE ARE WORSE THINGS THAN BEANS

I looked at my plate and grimaced. Then I looked at Will and grimaced again. He was eating the beans.

I picked up one of the evil vegetables and nibbled it. Disappointingly, space-beans tasted just like Earth-beans. I hid the rest of the vegetable under my leg, then looked around to see if anyone had noticed.

They had.

"My dear child," said Mother. "Aren't you going to eat?"

I smiled at the little snail. She really did seem very kind. "I don't really like beans," I explained.

The shadow behind the throne leant forward and whispered to Mother, who nodded. "I would very much appreciate it if you would eat," said the snail, in a voice that was just a little less melodic and a little more threatening. "In fact, I insist."

"But…" I said.

"EAT THE BEANS!"
screeched the snail.

"OR I'M GONNA HAVE ME
FIRE
LIZARD
GRILL YA
LIKE A FORGOTTEN
SAUSAGE ON A
BARBECUE!"

I was so shocked I nearly fell off my stool.

Will coughed and wiped his mouth. "She won't eat beans," he said. "She hates them."

I nodded vigorously in agreement.

"She'd rather die than even nibble one," he added.

I froze mid-nod.

"She'd rather be roasted to charcoal, and then re-roasted to soot, than even lick one."

I was shaking my head now. "That's not true," I said.

"And she isn't afraid of anything," continued Will.

"Yes, I am," I said to the little snail. "Sometimes I think I'm afraid of almost everything."

The shadowy figure of the ADVISOR leant in to whisper to the snail again.

"She'd happily fight every last slug on this ship," said Will.

"I wouldn't," I assured Fairy-Petal and Kitten-

Cuddles, who were leering terrifyingly at me. "I definitely wouldn't."

"And she'd win too," said Will. "She's ferocious. She once defeated a whole gang of **PIRATES**, and their pathetic leader."

In the shadows, the ADVISOR's hooded head snapped around to look at Will.

My brother smiled. "Isn't that right, *McSnottbeard*?"

BACK FROM THE DEAD

The ADVISOR pushed his hood back a little to reveal a face bristling with an equal amount of beard and menace. "Hello, yarrrrr wee cod snots."

Here are the top five reasons I hoped I would never see *McSnottbeard* again:

Things Worth Knowing No. 7
by Emilie

1) He smells.

2) He has a habit of singing songs that stink as badly as he does.

3) He wanted to kill me.

4) And that was before I was responsible for him being struck by lightning, falling off a massive tower and plunging down a humungous cliff into a furious sea.

5) He definitely isn't the type to forgive and forget.

The **PIRATE** stepped out from behind the throne and into the light. He was uglier than I remembered.

"What happened to your nose?" I asked.

"Fell on it," said *McSnottbeard*, fixing me with a particularly hateful look. "From a very high tower."

"Sorry about that," I said.

"You will be," growled the **PIRATE**.

I ducked down behind my plate of beans. "How did you know he was here?" I whispered to Will.

"Old trainers, dead fish and cat wee," said Will.

The smell! I should have recognized it. The stink of a **PIRATE** is something you don't easily forget. They never wash and only wipe their bums on their birthdays. Their stench is strong enough to kill most small animals.

Except, apparently, my cat.

"Hello," said Eiffel, poking his head out of *McSnottbeard*'s sleeve.

THE PROBLEM
WITH CATS

Some people say you can't trust cats. They are
wrong (and usually the sort of people you find
walking dogs). Cats are 100% trustworthy, so long
as you are trusting them to do what is best for
themselves.

"Eiffel!" I shouted happily.

"What are you doing with the **PIRATE**?"
Will asked suspiciously. "You're meant to be on
our side!"

My brother is a bit of a dog person.

Eiffel looked confused. "Really?" he said. "But
you're losing."

I looked around at the thousands of slugs staring
angrily at us. "He has a point," I said to Will.

"And the **PIRATE** has the people that feed me," continued Eiffel.

I was shocked by the cat's betrayal, but not half as shocked as I was to discover that *McSnottbeard* had our parents.

"Where?" I cried.

McSnottbeard cackled in that way that only **PIRATES** (and my auntie Becky) can. He reached back and yanked the red curtain behind the throne. It fell away to reveal two big blocks of slime.

PARENT PRICE

I jumped to my feet. To my surprise my parents' eyes flicked towards me.

"Sweetheart," Mum mouthed silently. Dad smiled in that way people do when everything is miserable but they are trying to make you feel better.

"Give them back!" Will shouted.

"No," said the **PIRATE**. "They're mine. I paid heaps for 'em. In fact you could say they cost the world."

McSnottbeard winked.

Will and I looked at each other in confusion.

"It's a play on words, ye dolphin droppings," growled the **PIRATE**. "Means I paid a lot for 'em, only in this case I really did pay the world."

"I don't get it," said Will.

McSnottbeard groaned. "I told the slugs they could eat the earth if they snatched ya folks for me. It really isn't funny if ye have to explain it."

"You swapped the planet for our parents?" I asked.

McSnottbeard smiled and nodded.

I frowned. "Why?"

"Aaaaar was hoping you'd ask," said the **PIRATE**. He raised a hand and clicked his fingers.

The arena went dark except for a spotlight into which *McSnottbeard* strode. Eiffel hissed, leaped to the ground and disappeared under the throne as the **PIRATE** shrugged off his robe to reveal a glittering jumpsuit. Then, to my absolute horror, *McSnottbeard* produced a microphone.

"Oh cripes!" I said. "He's going to sing."

PIRATES CAN'T SING

McSnottbeard tapped the microphone then pointed at me.

"This one goes out to some particularly 'orrible bilge burbs from the-soon-to-be-former-planet Earth."

"Cover your ears," said Will.

"There's nothing sadder in the universe than a PIRATE without a crew.

With no scurvy gang to man the sails there's nothing much to do.

It's been months since I have pillaged and it's left me feeling blue.

So I set out to fix my life and get even with you too.

A buccaneer needs two key things and one's linked to the other,

The first is a reputation which you ruined with your brother.

I was feared across the seven seas when I stole your dad and mother.

But you spoiled my fame and destroyed my name and now I need another.

— 143 —

Without a mob a PIRATE king is just a smelly sailor.

After falling off that tower my friends considered me a failure.

No PIRATE's going to join my ship just for my snazzy tailor.

But this I vow to you right now is revenge that I will savour.

And yes, I admit, I paid a bit to reverse my fall from grace.

I promised slugs could eat the world if they helped me save some face.

But I've found myself a little moon that can double as a base.

And I'll miss the earth but I'll get me kicks by pirating in space."

McSnottbeard ended by wiggling his hips, whirling his arms then bowing.

There wasn't a clap in the entire arena. Though to be fair, that may have been due to the slugs' overwhelming lack of arms.

WORLDLY WORRIES

Here are five things you should know about
PIRATES' plans.

Things Worth Knowing No. 8
by Emilie

1) PIRATES' plans don't have to
make sense so long as they are nasty.

2) And they are always nasty.

3) They often involve gold coins (called
doubloons). Or senseless destruction.
Typically both.

4) PIRATES like to tell you what they are planning. It isn't confessing, it's boasting.

5) They will also always leave you a map. That's just a thing with PIRATES.

Will raised his hand.

"What is it, ya wee sprat spit?" growled *McSnottbeard*.

"If you destroy the earth who's going to know you re-kidnapped our parents?"

"Details." The **PIRATE** shrugged.

Will put his hand up again. He seemed to have mistaken the colosseum for a classroom.

"Have you told the slugs about the oceans?" he asked.

"The what?" said *McSnottbeard*.

"You know, the Pacific, the Arctic, the Atlantic and the other two."

"Indian and Southern," said the **PIRATE**, whose one redeeming quality appeared to be oceanography.

Will nodded. "And the seas."

McSnottbeard looked puzzled. "What about them?"

"They cover 71% of the planet."

"So?"

"What are they full of?" said Will.

There was a long pause as *McSnottbeard* thought.

And thought.

...

And thought.

...

And thought.

...

And thought.

...

And thought.

...

And thought.

For so long it started to get embarrassing.

...

He thought some more.

...

And more.

...

And more.

...

And more.

I decided to help out. "Is it fish?"

My brother rolled his eyes and
shook his head.

"Dolphins," I suggested.

Will looked at me dumbfounded.

"They aren't fish," I said.

"You aren't helping," said Will.

"Doubloons?" said *McSnottbeard* hopefully.

PIRATES really love doubloons.

Will shook his head.

"Sea slugs," suggested Fairy-Petal.

"They live in oceans and the sea."

I nodded. "Their name is misleading."

Will put his head in his hands.

"Doubloons?" repeated *McSnottbeard*.

"Stop guessing!" groaned Will.

"It's doubloons, isn't it?"

"NO!" yelled Will. "It's SALT!"

Around the arena tens of thousands of alien slug monsters simultaneously gasped with a sound like a vacuum cleaner sucking up a wet chicken. Every eye on every stalk of every slug stared angrily at the **PIRATE**.

"Is that true?" asked Mother. "Is 71% of the earth salty?"

"Hmmmm," said the **PIRATE**, looking suddenly shifty. "Course not."

Mother didn't look convinced.

"Or perhaps it is," said *McSnottbeard*. "Arrrr guess you'll have to find out for ye selves."

Then he raised his hand and clicked his fingers. For a second I thought he was going to sing again, so I was relieved when he threw the microphone away.

That relief lasted as long as it took for the roof of the colosseum to shatter as a **PIRATE** ship crashed through it.

DUMB THINGS

Dads say dumb things. For example, when you point out your brother isn't eating his vegetables, they'll say, "People in glass houses shouldn't throw stones."

What those people really shouldn't do is walk around naked.

Or, when you get back after a holiday, they'll say, "There's no place like home", when there clearly is because you can see it.

But the most stupid thing they say is "It's raining cats and dogs", when what they really mean is that it's pouring with rain. That's not only dumb, it's dangerous, because a kid might go outside to try to find a pet when all they're going to get is a cold.

I only mention this so you know, when I tell you it rained glass and **PIRATES**, I really mean it rained glass and **PIRATES**.

RAIN AND PAIN

It rained glass and **PIRATES**.

The **PIRATES** slid down ropes from the flying galleon. The glass just fell.

"Move!" shouted my brother as he shoved me under the table.

Huge shards of glass twanged as they cut our stools in two. A second later heavy boots crushed what remained of our seats as the **PIRATES** hit the ground.

Will and I rolled away and ended up next to Mother, who was sitting on her throne with one eye wide with horror and the other

squinting with rage. Nearby Kitten-Cuddles and Fairy-Petal roared, and possibly rushed to

fight the **PIRATES**, though with the speed
that slugs move it was hard to say.

The **PIRATES**, on the other hand,
moved quickly and with a jerky precision. In
a flash, one had popped a space helmet over
McSnottbeard's head, while others toppled my
parents' slime blocks and attached them to the
PIRATE ship with ropes.

"Hang on," I whispered to Will. "Didn't we
just survive a song about how *McSnottbeard*
has no **PIRATE** crew?"

"They aren't **PIRATES**," said Will.

"They look like **PIRATES**,"
I said.

"Look closer."

So I did.

"Are they...?"

"B.U.R.P.s,"
said Will.

AAAAR!2DIE2

RISKYPEDIA
The Adventurer's Enclyclopedia

>> B.U.R.P.s
Blooming Unpleasant Robot PIRATES, or
B.U.R.P.s, were created by the mad
scientist Whats Thisdo in her laboratory
on the planet Ka-BOOM. Thisdo worked for
decades to make the robots ever more
evil and lethal, which possibly explains
her last journal entry before she died:
"I believe the B.U.R.P. is the most
dangerous machine ever created. I am
just going to turn it on."

I popped my head above the table to get a better
look at the robots.

"Are they really that dangerous?" I asked Will. A laser blast ripped through my hair, leaving a hole. I ducked back down. "You don't have to answer that," I said.

McSnottbeard and the B.U.R.P.s leapt aboard the slime blocks, as the **PIRATE** ship reversed out of the hole in the roof and lifted them into the air.

"See ya later, seal snots!" *McSnottbeard* yelled down to us. "And by later, I mean never."

For the second time that day Will and I watched helplessly as our parents floated away. Only this time our cat was going with them.

Eiffel's head poked over the edge of one of the blocks of slime. He looked down at me, and though I couldn't be sure, I thought I saw him wink.

GOING, GOING...

"They're gone," I said to no one in particular.

"Uh huh," said Will, staring up at the hole in the roof.

"Our parents," I said.

"Yep."

"And the cat."

"That fleabag traitor," said Will. "Good riddance."

"We lost," I said.

"Nope."

"What?"

"Look," said Will. "We know who has our parents, don't we?"

"I guess," I said.

"And we know why he snatched them."

"OK."

"We know they're alive."

"Sure."

"And we know where they are."

"We do?"

"*McSnottbeard*'s hideout," said Will.

"Which is on a moon," I said.

Will gave me a thumbs-up.

"An unknown moon, orbiting an unknown planet, in any of the trillions of galaxies in the universe," I said.

Will nodded. "You are forgetting rule number five."

"Number five?"

"From your list of things worth knowing about **PIRATES**' plans," said Will. "They always leave a map. We just have to find it."

Behind me I heard the skin-crawling noise of someone eating loudly.

McMAIL

I turned to Fairy-Petal. A piece of wet paper
hung out of the slug's mouth.

"NO!" Will yelled. He leapt at the slug and snatched the soggy sheet.

"Is that…?" I asked.

Will looked at the paper in his hands. "It was the map," he sighed as he shoved the scrap in his pocket.

mcsnottbeard@aaarghoo.pir8

From the throne next to us came a regal cough. "Well that was unfortunate," Mother said. "Still. We shouldn't let it ruin the entertainment."

A cheer went up from the slugs.

"Entertainment?" I asked.

"She's going to feed us to the fire lizard," said Will.

"But…" I surveyed the shattered glass, broken stools and scattered beans. "Don't you want to help us get *McSnottbeard*?" I asked Mother.

The snail thought for a second. "No."

TOOTHY, WINGED AND AS BIG AS A BUS

Mother, Fairy-Petal and Kitten-Cuddles had taken seats in the front row of the colosseum.

Will and I stood facing each other in the middle of the arena.

"What's happening?" I asked my brother.

"I think we are waiting for the fire lizard," said Will.

"Oh."

We waited.

"Will," I said eventually. "What does a fire lizard look like?"

Will shrugged. "Never seen one."

"I think it might be big."

"Could be."

"Probably about as big as a bus?"

"Perhaps," said Will.

 "Huge teeth?" I asked.

"Probably."

 "Wings?"

"I doubt it."

"Smoke curling out of its nose?"

"That would make sense given the fire," said Will.

I nodded. "I think you're wrong about the wings."

"Why?"

I pointed over Will's shoulder where a large door had slid open. Out of it emerged a bus-sized lizard, with huge teeth and smoke curling out of its nose.

And it had wings.

OUT OF THE FRYING PAN, INTO THE FIRE (LIZARD)

The fire lizard blinked as it walked into the light. Then it stretched its neck, extended its wings and roared.

Or more precisely, it

It was so loud I didn't so much hear it as feel it. And what I mostly felt was the urge to run.

That turned out to be the wrong thing to do.

The moment Will and I moved the fire lizard turned towards us and let out a blast of flame.

The slugs cheered wildly and wetly.

Will and I skidded to a halt on the opposite side of the arena, our hair gently smoking.

"That," I puffed, "isn't a lizard. It's a DRAGON!"

"I know!" said Will, with a huge smile on his face.

"Why are you smiling?"

"It's a real, live dragon!"

"So?"

"So!" said Will. "So if dragons are real, think what else might exist. There could be unicorns, flying monkeys…"

"I am more worried about what might cease to exist in here," I said.

Will shrugged. "I wouldn't worry. Dragons are blind, or near enough. As long as we don't move we'll be fine."

"How can you possibly know that?" I asked. "You didn't even know dragons existed a second ago!"

"Saw it in *Lava Lizards 4*," said Will. "Dragons get so much smoke in their eyes they can barely see anything."

LAVA LIZARDS 4

THE STORY DRAG(S)ON

I looked at the dragon. It was blinking and squinting.

"So I just stand still?"

"Nope."

"What?"

"You need to get its attention so I can pop this into its mouth." Will reached into his pyjama pocket and pulled out a bottle of Soapernova Death Bubbles.

"Where'd you get that?"

"Page one hundred and ten," said Will.

THIS CHAPTER IS EMBARRASSING

Will lay on the ground between me and the dragon. It had taken him about twenty minutes to get there, moving with all the electrifying pace of an alien slug monster so as to avoid being noticed by the dragon.

Meanwhile, I had been standing very still.

The dragon had wandered around at first, every so often eating a bean from the arena floor, before it got bored and sat down in the middle of the stadium to bite its toes.

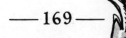

Talking of bored, the slugs weren't happy. They were booing and there was the occasional shout of "Run around", which was ironic.

"OK!" Will called to me. "Now move, but also stay there. I need it to walk over me to get to you."

I waved my arms half-heartedly. To be honest, I wasn't that keen to get the attention of a murderous, fire-breathing monster.

I needn't have worried. The dragon was so focused on its toes it didn't notice me. I tried yelling, but it turns out dragons are more or less deaf as well as blind. Eventually, I looked over at Will and shrugged.

"Dance around!" he shouted.

Reluctantly, really, really reluctantly, I began to dance.

An Explanation About My Dance
by Emilie

1) Maya from my school thinks she is a pop star.

← MAYA: DEFINITELY NOT A POP STAR!

2) Because she thinks she is a pop star she thinks she needs backing dancers.

3) Because I am Maya's friend I am, unfortunately, one of those dancers.

4) The dance that Maya makes me do involves hopping on the spot while flapping my arms.

5) It is so bad I have given it a secret name.

"What are you doing?" asked Will.

"The 'Boogaloo Chicken'," I shouted back as I hopped and flapped.

"It's awful," he said.

"I know," I puffed.

The dragon turned towards me.

"It's working," said Will.

Flames snorted out of the dragon's nose as it stood up.

"I can't believe I am saying this," said Will, "but keep going."

I Boogaloo Chickened harder than I had ever Boogaloo Chickened before – which, given my limited enthusiasm for the dance, wasn't difficult.

The dragon roared and lumbered in my direction. The slugs let out a huge cheer, potentially for my dancing, but probably for the dragon.

ROASTED CHICKEN?

The ground trembled as the dragon approached. Every bit of me wanted to run. None of me wanted to dance. But I danced.

The dragon took another step. It was nearly over my brother now and certainly close enough to barbecue me.

"Will!" I shouted as I flapped. "Now!"

There was a rumble like the sound of a forest fire deep in the dragon's belly. It breathed deeply, filling its lungs. Flames licked out of its nostrils. Its jaws

opened and the rumble of distant fire grew into a roaring inferno.

"WILLIAM!!!" I screamed. "NOWWWWW!"

Will sprang to his feet, grabbed the dragon's bottom jaw, and threw the soap into its mouth. The dragon's teeth snapped shut, just missing my brother's hand.

Confusion flashed in the dragon's eyes.

Then it hiccupped.

Bubbles floated out of its nose and popped with little puffs of smoke.

Will scrambled from beneath the dragon, seconds before it crashed to the ground. Around the arena the cheering slugs fell silent.

"What's happening?" I asked Will.

"It's filling up with bubbles," he said. "Heavy ones."

The dragon burped a particularly large and smoky bubble then groaned miserably.

"We won," I said.

Will nodded.

I was so excited I did a little Boogaloo
Chicken to celebrate.

NOT BETTER

In most stories things get better after a dragon is defeated. Heroes are celebrated. They usually get a stack of gold, and in fairy tales there's always a royal wedding.

That's not what happens in this story, which might be for the best given the royalty on offer.

"Pathetic primates!" Mother shouted from on top of a large satellite dish that had been lowered into the arena. "You broke our lizard!"

"We won," said Will. "Now you have to help us find *McSnottbeard*."

"Won?" Fairy-Petal poked its head out from behind the dish. "You don't

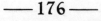

win after-dinner entertainment. You ruined the show!"

Behind us the dragon burped more bubbles and whimpered. The slugs in the seats around the arena booed.

Mother surveyed the angry crowd. "There's gonna be a riot if we don't blinkin' well do something." Her posh accent had completely disappeared. She sounded like my dad when he watches football.

"Do something?" I said. "Like what?"

"Standing just there should be fine," said Fairy-Petal.

The slug made a noise like a drain clearing, then spat an enormous throaty gob of slime over mine and Will's feet.

TRANSMOGRI-WHATS-IT

"Urghhh!" I groaned. I tried to pull my feet free but I was stuck to the floor.

"That's a quantum transmogrifier," said Will, looking at the satellite dish.

I stared at him blankly.

"It transmogrifies physical matter into quantum data for reassembly at a remote location," said Will. "I saw it in *Machine Man 3: Critical System Failure*."

HE IS BACK!!!
And this time you can't control him...

MACHINE·MAN·3

I shook my head. "I was with you right up until you started speaking."

"It emails people," Will said, rolling his eyes.

"You could have just said that." I stuck out my tongue.

Fairy-Petal pressed a button on the machine with one of his eyes. The dish began to hum.

"One sincerely hopes to never see you again," said Mother in her posh accent. "And if I do I'll rip your bloomin' heads off," she added in her football-dad voice.

"Have fun." Fairy-Petal smirked in a way that suggested that there wasn't going to be much fun to be had.

A ball of blue light appeared at the centre of the dish and began to expand toward us.

"Cool!" said Will.

Then there was a flash...

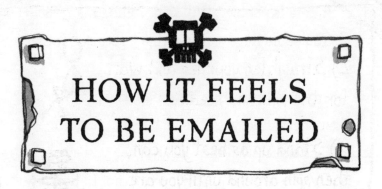

HOW IT FEELS TO BE EMAILED

You are probably wondering what it feels like to be emailed.

The good news is you can experience it for yourself by following my five-step guide to recreating how it feels to be emailed:

Five-Step Guide to Recreating How it Feels to be Emailed
by Emilie

1) Sit on the floor on top of one of your legs until it goes completely numb.

2) Straighten your leg and wait for the pins and needles.

3) Stand up as best you can, then spin around until you are dizzy.

4) Lie on the ground and try to imagine the tingling in your leg covers your entire body and that the world is turning twice as fast.

5) Be thankful you've never been emailed.

YOU AM I

I was lying on a cold stone floor.

Normally that would be bad. But at that moment it was the best thing I had going for me. For one, it wasn't spinning, unlike the rest of the world. And two, it was so cold that the bits of me touching it had lost feeling. The rest of me felt like it was under attack from electric wasps.

I put my hands out to hold the room still and touched an arm.

"William?"

"Uh huh," said my brother.

"I'm dying," I croaked deeply.

"Full-body quantum transmission," said Will in a high-pitched voice. "That's the coolest thing ever."

I shook my head feebly. "Worst thing ever."

My voice sounded wrong. It was too low.
I coughed to clear it.

"You mean the spinning and the pins and
needles?" squeaked Will. "You need to sit up."

"Nope. Don't want to make the wasps angry."

A few seconds passed.

"What's wrong with your voice?" piped Will.
"What's wrong with my voice?" he added.

We both sat up and looked at each other.

Or … rather, ourselves.

Or … well, it was complicated.

THE OLD SWITCHEROO

Sitting on the floor next to me was me.

"Wow!" said the me that wasn't me. "Full-body quantum transmission with a cerebral displacement glitch."

That was definitely Will. No one else makes that little sense.

"What happened?!"

Will made a don't-be-thick face, but with my face, which was disturbing. "I just told you. Full-body quantum transmission with a cere—"

"English!" I shouted, and then immediately felt bad for telling myself off.

"There was a mistake," said Will. "My brain ended up in your body. And vice-versa."

I looked down at myself. What I saw was Will's body leading down to Will's legs in Will's pyjamas. I pulled out the waistband.

"Stop that!" shouted Will.

"AHHHHH!" I screamed, letting the elastic snap back.

"Never do that again!"

I nodded.

"Ever!"

I nodded again as I stood. "Wow! You are tall!" I said. "I can see everything from up here."

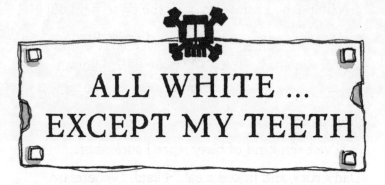

ALL WHITE ...
EXCEPT MY TEETH

There wasn't much to see. We were in a small
room with white walls and a white ceiling.
There was a white door in one wall, and a
white bunk bed with white sheets against
another. In the corner of the room was a desk
and a chair, and I bet you can guess what colour
they were.

The only interesting things in the whole
room were some posters on the wall. And they
were only slightly better than the white paint.

Will pushed himself up off the floor, held out my arms, looked at my hands, then jumped up and down a few times. "You are light," he said. Then he grimaced. "You could do with brushing your teeth."

"I've been kind of busy since I sucked on Dad's sock and licked a cat," I said. "Where are we?"

Will rubbed my fingers over my teeth as he walked to the desk. He picked up a sheet of paper. "We're in a vegetable mine."

"A what?"

"A ... vegetable ... mine," Will said slowly.

"I ... heard ... you," I replied. "It still doesn't make sense. You don't mine vegetables."

"Welcome to Alfalfa-Centauri, home of the universe's premier vegetable mine," Will read from the paper. "Congratulations on your new positions as valued employees and despised prisoners. We hope you enjoy your stay – it'll be a long one."

I felt like crying.

OK, I cried.

Will came over and tried to put his arm around my shoulder, but had to settle for my waist when he realized how much taller I was.

"It'll be OK," he said, though I noticed he was sniffling a little too.

I nodded, rubbed my nose and wiped my eyes. "It's just that I could do with seeing a friendly face that isn't mine," I said.

And no sooner had I said it than a small panel slid open in the door.

"Room thervice," said a voice from the other side.

THUPRITHE!

Staring at me through the panel was the sort of face that would not only make you scream if you saw it in the dark, but would make you wish it was darker. The face was so hideous that a monster could have worn it to scare its friends at Halloween.

And it was smiling at me.

And this might surprise you, but I was smiling back.

You see, that horrible face was both familiar and friendly. "Hello, Yeth!" I said.

"Mathter William," said the face, its unstitched eye lighting up with happiness. "Now thith ith a thurprithe."

I was confused for a moment. "Oh no," I said. "I'm Emilie. It's a long story but we swapped bodies. That's William," I added, pointing at my brother.

"Oh thuper!" said the igor. "You know, we are always thwapping bodieth back where I come from. Or bitth of them at least."

Here are five things you should know about igors:

Things Worth Knowing No. 9
by Emilie

1) Igors generally turn up in the most unlikely places. Though I guess that makes unlikely places the most likely places they will turn up.

2) Igors are super nice, though an igor would probably describe itself as thuper nithe.

3) Igors always thpeak like thith, which makes them impossible to understand — at least for me.

4) The igor at the door is called Stitches, but due to an ongoing misunderstanding I call him Yeth.

5) The last time I saw Yeth he was working for an evil wizard and helped feed me to zombies. I was upset at the time, but I forgave him.

HELP WANTED

Yeth held up a plate. "I brought you a thnack," he said.

"Thnack?" I asked. Somehow I could understand cats, snails and slugs but I still couldn't understand Yeth.

"A snack," translated Will.

"Oh great!" I said. "I'm starving."

The igor pushed the plate through the hole in the door and my heart sank.

"Beans," I whimpered.

Yeth's smile faded into a look of such disappointment that I actually felt bad for not liking beans. I changed the subject. "What are you doing here?"

"Therving you thupper," said the igor cheerfully.

"She means on this planet," said my brother.

"Working," said Yeth. "I anthered an ad for a jailer in the New Yuck Times."

I looked to Will for help.

"He is in charge of the prison," said Will.

Yeth smiled proudly.

"Does that mean you have keys?" I asked.

"Oh yeth." The igor nodded and held up a ring of keys. "It'th a very rethponth ... rethponthib ... important job."

I was stunned.

"You can let us out," I squealed, only in Will's voice. It came out much deeper than I was expecting.

THTUCK

Will and I sat on the bunk bed in our prison cell.

"Why wouldn't he let us out?" I asked.

"He is an igor."

"He's also meant to be my friend."

Will shrugged. "Igors do what they are told to do. That's what makes an igor an igor. That and the spare body parts."

"But what if that means doing something horrible?"

"Your 'friend' works for alien slug monsters," said Will. "Horrible is basically his job description."

I thought about it for a second and then lay back on the bed. "Well I don't believe that," I said. "I think people can choose the kind of people they want to be. Even if they are igors and not actually people."

Will grabbed a pillow from the top bunk and lay down next to me. It was surprising how little room he took up now he was in my body.

"That would be nice." Will yawned. "But if it was true, we'd have the keys."

I was still thinking about that when I heard snoring from next to me. Will had fallen asleep.

Great, I thought as my own eyes closed. *Not only am I stuck in prison, but it turns out I snore.*

VEGETABLES ARE GOOD FOR YOU

I don't know how long I slept for, but it was long enough for Yeth to have snuck in with another meal.

Thankfully there were no beans, though it wasn't exactly candy floss either. There were carrots, cucumbers, lettuce and, rather depressingly, Brussels Sprouts. I hate sprouts almost as much as beans.

There was also a card.

Dear Emilie,
A tHelection of vegetables for you.
The carrotth are for youR eyes,
cucumber for your thkin and the lettuth
is the <u>KEY</u> to happineth.
watch out For wormth!

I picked up a cucumber and bit into it with a crunch that woke Will.

"Morning. Or at least I think it's morning. It's hard to tell without a window," I said. "You should eat – I don't want me wasting away."

Will rolled out of bed, yawned with my mouth, then picked up a carrot and walked over to the door.

He rattled the handle then studied the lock. "If we had a bit of cardboard I might be able to open this."

I held up Yeth's note. "Like this?"

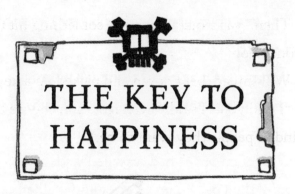

THE KEY TO HAPPINESS

Will began to fold the message. Then stopped.

"Did you read this?" he asked.

I nodded. "Don't worry. I checked the vegetables for worms."

"Lettuce is the key to happiness," mumbled Will as he picked up the huge head of lettuce from the plate.

"Yeah, I didn't really underst—"

Will ripped the lettuce in half.

"I was going to eat that!" I said.

There was a metallic *ting* as something hit the stone floor.

Will smiled, bent down and picked up a key.

"I told you!" I said. "Even igors can choose the kind of people they want to be."

This key belongs to igor.

THERE ARE WORSE THINGS THAN SLIME

Vegetable mines aren't nice places. It's not the vegetables – though the beans sticking out of the walls don't help. It's more the smell, the darkness and the confusing tunnels.

And the slime, which covered the walls and pooled ankle-deep on the floor. For some reason there's a lot of slime in this book.

"Which way?" I asked Will as we stepped out of our room and into a dimly lit tunnel.

"When in doubt, follow the sprout," said my brother, gesturing to a line of Brussels Sprouts laid out on the floor.

We followed the vegetable trail, stepping carefully around the deepest puddles of ooze, until we came to a junction. An arrow made out of beans pointed away to the right.

"I guess it's that way," I said.

"How do we know it isn't a trap?" asked Will.

Beyond the arrow was a message spelled out in sprouts.

"That's reassuring," said Will.

In the distance there was a faint roar, like the sound of a train passing.

"That's not," I said.

"Might be the wind," suggested Will.

There was another roar, closer and louder. It started to our left, shook the tunnel as it passed under us, then disappeared to our right.

"Strong wind," I said. "Let's get moving."

As we walked another rumbling noise began to build. It was so quiet that at first it was just part of the background. And it grew so slowly that neither of us realized it was there until the tunnel began to shake.

Then the wind started.

In the darkness behind us something massive moved.

"What was—" I began.

"RUN!" screamed Will, sprinting past me.

I ran.

I ran faster than I had ever run – partly because I was really scared, but mostly because of Will's long legs.

I passed myself, or rather Will, in just a few strides.

But as quick as I was, whatever was making the noise was quicker.

WORMS!

I should have kept running.

That would have been sensible. But sensible isn't always my strong point. So instead I did the other thing that people do when something is behind them.

I did the thing you shouldn't do.

I stopped and looked.

And because I looked, Will looked too.

And this is what we saw!

Yeth's message flashed back into my mind:

watch out For wormth!

I pulled Will forward.
"They weren't in the
vegetables. They're
in the tunnels!"

WORM FOOD

We ran again. Faster this time.

But still not fast enough.

The worm gained, until it was close enough
for us to hear its skin sliding moistly against the
walls of the tunnel.

Ahead, in the dim light, I saw a small cave in
the wall.

"There!" I shouted, turning to make sure Will
had seen it.

And that was the second mistake I made in
that tunnel.

You see, if I hadn't looked at Will I would have
seen the puddle. And if I'd seen it I wouldn't have
fallen into it. And if I hadn't fallen, my brother
wouldn't have tripped over me.

We hit the puddle with a splash. I skidded on my stomach to the far edge and scrambled to my feet just next to the cave opening. Will had landed in the deepest part of the slime. He stood then slipped and fell again.

Behind him the worm's massive mouth loomed with teeth like long swords.

"WILL!" I screamed.

Will's eyes – my eyes – looked up at me with horror.

"JUMP!" he yelled as the worm closed on him.

So I jumped.

ALONE (ISH)

The worm crashed past, like a train – a particularly wet train.

Slime splashed everywhere, leaving me rubbing sticky globs out of my eyes. Carefully, with a horrible sense of dread, I poked my head out of the cave.

I expected to see Will smeared down the walls in a terrible soup – 50% slime and 50% my own body – so I was relieved to find the tunnel empty.

Then another awful thought hit me.

"It ate him," I whispered.

I slumped back against the wall. Tears sprung to my eyes.

"This is all wrong," I sobbed. "I'm just a kid. I should be climbing trees with friends, not alone in a mine full of monsters."

I rubbed my eyes and looked down at my wet hands – my brother's hands.

I took a deep breath. *Will wouldn't cry*, I thought, though I had a nagging suspicion he probably would. *He would get up and keep going.*

I clenched my fists.

"Perhaps I'm only a kid," I said. "But I am a kid who thinks people can choose what kind of people they want to be. And I choose to be the kind of kid who keeps on going. I choose to be the kind of kid that escapes vegetable mines, defeats **PIRATES** and saves parents ... even if she has to do it alone and in a boy's body."

"OK." I stood up. "Let's go then."

And I would have too. But, just at that moment, a hand punched through the wall and grabbed my shoulder.

ON THE OTHER HAND

I screamed.

And after that I screamed some more.

I probably would have continued screaming too, but a second hand punched through the wall and clamped over my mouth.

My "AAAAARGH!" became a "GMMMF!" and then a "OWWW!" as the hands pulled me hard against the wall.

I heard a crack.

Then there was an even louder crack.

And then the wall collapsed. I fell back into darkness.

COWSUIT
CLARINET

Actually, it wasn't completely dark.

I could just make out that I was in a very low cave and on the far side of it there was a faint glow.

In that dim light was something so unlikely, so breathtakingly incomprehensible, so absolutely mind-bogglingly unfathomable, so... Well, you get the idea. I would have been less surprised if I had discovered my teacher, Miss Lorraine, wearing a cowsuit and playing a punk rock rendition of *Silent Night* on a baguette.

ALIVE AND CLICKING

Things I Didn't Expect to See No. 1
by Emilie

1) A young girl.

2) A young girl who looked like me.

3) A young girl who looked like
me but was actually my brother.

4) A young girl who looked like me but was actually my brother sitting at a computer.

5) A young girl who looked like me but was actually my brother sitting at a computer rather than being digested in the stomach of a giant worm.

HOW?

"William?" I asked hesitantly.

"Yep," said Will, tapping on the keyboard.

"But … I saw you, or me, or…" I babbled.
"I saw us get eaten!"

Will turned around. "No you didn't."

"In the tunnel." I shuddered at the memory.
"There was the worm. And all those teeth.
You couldn't get out of the slime puddle."

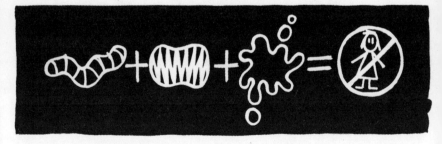

"And then you jumped," said Will. "You never
actually saw me get eaten."

That was true.

"Yeth pulled me through the ground,"
said Will. "He pulled you through the wall too."

"Yeth?" I said uncertainly.

A smiling and poorly-stitched face emerged
from the darkness beside me. "Thurprithe,"
it said.

I jumped about a foot in the air, cracked
my head on the roof of the cave and knocked
myself out for the second time in this book.

VEGEZOMBIES

I woke to see Yeth's patchwork face staring
down at me. He was holding a
wrench and an umbrella.

"What are you doing?" I asked.

"I am watching you lie on the
ground," said Yeth. Igors are
very literal.

"I mean what are you
doing with my brother, an
umbrella and a wrench?"

"We are conthr ... conthruct
... building a transmogrifier."

I sat up and rubbed the lump on the top of
my head. "Why?" I asked, though I feared I
already knew the answer.

"I think I can email us to *McSnottbeard*'s moon base," said Will.

"You think?"

"Well, I'm having some trouble with the quantum coding but I am getting the hang of it."

"At least you didn't just see it in a film," I said.

Will smiled my own smile at me. "*Hacker Horror III: Desktop of Doom.*"

I looked at him in disbelief.

"Is there any film you haven't seen?"

Will shrugged.

"How do you know where to send us?" I asked.

"I don't," Will said. "But in your pocket, or my pocket really, is the bit of paper I saved from the slug. And on it is *McSnottbeard*'s email address."

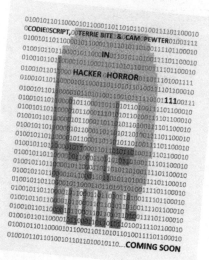

INTER-NOT!

There was no way I was going to be emailed again and I let Will know.

"You could stay here," he said.

"OK!"

"What?"

"OK," I repeated. "It isn't so bad here. I could get used to eating vegetables."

"Really?" said Will.

"And I have Yeth for a friend."

The igor's face split into a grin so wide that it nearly touched the back of his head.

"Even if I can't understand him."

The smile disappeared.

"And I bet the worms aren't even that dangerous once you get the knack of avoiding them."

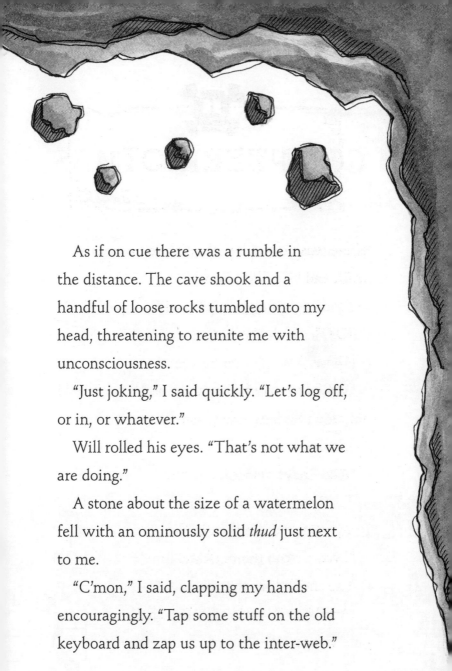

As if on cue there was a rumble in the distance. The cave shook and a handful of loose rocks tumbled onto my head, threatening to reunite me with unconsciousness.

"Just joking," I said quickly. "Let's log off, or in, or whatever."

Will rolled his eyes. "That's not what we are doing."

A stone about the size of a watermelon fell with an ominously solid *thud* just next to me.

"C'mon," I said, clapping my hands encouragingly. "Tap some stuff on the old keyboard and zap us up to the inter-web."

COMPUTER GAMES

"So you can use the email address to send us to *McSnottbeard*'s computer?" I asked Will as a blue light began to glow at the tip of the umbrella that Yeth had attached to the computer. "Won't that be squashy?"

"We will be digitized," said Will. "But only for a bit before we are reassembled on *McSnottbeard*'s moon."

"Oh," I said. "Cool."

The light grew bigger.

"Will," I said. "What's digitized?"

And then there was a flash.

And then another flash.

And then…

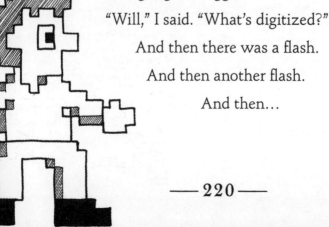

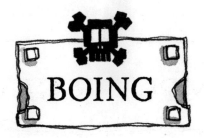

BOING

"WHAT HAPPENED!?" I yelled.

"It worked," said Will.

"We are made out of boxes!"

"Pixels," said Will. "We are inside
McSnottbeard's computer system."

I looked down at my boxy legs, and at my
boxy dress and at my boxy hands, then back
at my boxy dress again. "Am I me?" I turned
to Will, who, if you ignored the sharp edges,
looked like himself. "You are you!"
I shouted.

"I switched us back," said Will.

I was so excited I jumped
in the air.

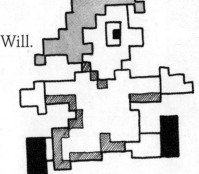

From all around us came an electronic *boing*.

"What was that?" I asked.

"It couldn't be..."

"What couldn't it be?"

"It sounded like the jump sound-effect from *Barrel Boing II: PIRATE Peril*," said Will.

"Another movie?"

Will shook his pixelated head. "A video game."

Things Worth Knowing No. 10
by Emilie

1) *Barrel Boing II: PIRATE Peril* was one of the first arcade games.

2) If you don't know what an arcade game is, ask your parents – it will make them feel very old.

3) The object of the game is to make your way up a series of ramps, while jumping over barrels and ducking fish that are thrown by a giant PIRATE standing at the exit.

4) To win you have to get out the exit.

5) No one ever wins. The game is impossible.

"So we are in a video game?" I asked.

Will shook his head. "Impossible," he said. "Anyway, if we were, there would be jangly music and a giant **PIRATE** up there." Will pointed to a spot just next to a door high above us – a spot where pixels suddenly began to appear.

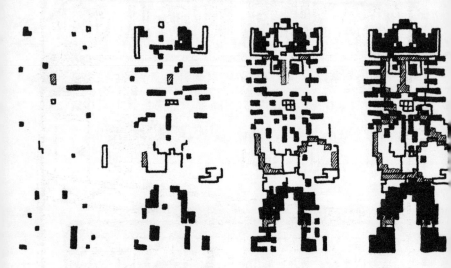

"A giant **PIRATE** like that?" I asked.

From all around and nowhere in particular jangly music started to play.

"And music like that?" I added.

My brother wasn't listening. He was staring at a line of massive white letters that had appeared in mid-air.

"Uh oh," said Will.

MARSHMALLOW NOSTRILS

The pixelated **PIRATE** let out a chilling, mechanical laugh. He was holding a barrel in one hand.

Will grabbed my shoulders. Despite his boxiness I could see he was worried. "The **PIRATE** will throw stuff at us," he said.

I nodded.

"You jump the barrels," said Will. "You duck the fish."

"Don't sweat it." I smiled. "It's a game. It's not like we could die."

Will shook his head. "The objects are digital. We are digital. If they hit you, you lose a life. And the thing about *Barrel Boing II*, the reason it is so famously impossible, is that you only get one life."

I looked at Will in disbelief. "So if something hits me…"

"Game over. That's why you need to do exactly what I say."

I shook my head. The last time I agreed to do what Will said I ended up at the doctor's with a nose full of marshmallows.

"No marshmallows this time," Will promised.

I thought for a second then nodded.

"Good," said Will. "JUMP!"

Will and I jumped with an electronic *boing* as a barrel rolled underneath us.

"Now run!" shouted my brother.

We ran up a ramp, past a ladder and arrived at a blank wall, which I realized was the edge of the screen. All the time the jangly music played.

Will turned back to me. "These old games all follow patterns," he said. "In *Barrel Boing II*, the **PIRATE** throws a barrel, a barrel, another barrel, a fish, a barrel, a fish and another fish. Then he starts over."

"Got it," I said. "Barrel, barrel, fish, barrel…"

Will shook his head. "Barrel, barrel, barrel, fish, barrel, fish, fish."

"OK," I said. "Three barrels, two fish…?"

Will rolled his eyes.

I stuck out my pixelated tongue. "Just shout jump or duck," I said. "I'll catch on."

 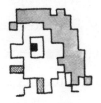

FURIOUS FOWL

We made our way up the ladder and along another ramp, ducking or jumping depending on whether we risked death by barrel or fish.

Once we reached the far side of the screen we stopped again.

"There are five levels, including the exit level," said Will. "So we are nearly halfway."

I gave him a thumbs-up. "Easy."

"It gets harder," said Will. "The game speeds up on each level. Also, there may be an angry goose."

"Sorry?" I said as I ducked a fish.

"If you jump or duck the goose you die. You have to wait for it to jump, then run underneath it. OK?"

I nodded. "What's it angry about?"

Will shrugged and took off up the ladder. I scrambled after him on to the next level and immediately jumped a barrel then ducked two fish. I made it two more steps before I had to jump again, then another step and another jump. The obstacles were coming faster.

Two platforms above us the **PIRATE** laughed evilly and electronically.

"No goose," I said, when we had made it to the far side of the level.

"Let's hope our luck holds." Will smiled. "You ready?"

I waited for a barrel to roll down the ladder. Then to prove how ready I was, I pushed in front of Will and climbed up to the level just below the **PIRATE**.

The barrels and fish were coming so fast there was barely time to move between jumping and ducking.

I was getting good at it though. Barrel – jump,

barrel – jump, fish – duck.

For the first time in my life I was actually enjoying a computer game.

Then I forgot to jump a barrel.

It was the goose's fault. I was jumping and ducking perfectly when there was an electronic honk and a bird popped into existence just in front of me.

"Goose!" I shouted. "Angry goose!" I added unnecessarily.

I ducked a fish and the goose lunged. It would have bitten me if Will hadn't dragged me back. "Remember," he said. "Don't duck or jump near the goose."

"Got it," I said as I backed up to put some space between me and the peeved poultry.

"Wait for it to jump then run," Will said.

I nodded. And just as I did the goose jumped.

I watched the bird rise into the air and I ran.

Which is why I didn't see the barrel until it was too late.

DIDN'T MENTION THAT!

One of the strange things about being in a video game (but not nearly the strangest) is what's missing. For example, there's no wind when you run, no weight when you jump and no impact when you land. You never even get tired.

You don't feel much of anything. Which was why I didn't feel the heat of the fireball as it flew past and exploded the barrel.

I stood stunned. I was alive. "How?" I said to myself.

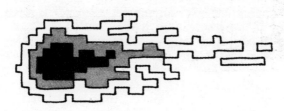

"Run!" said Will as he dashed past.

I ran. Behind us the goose came down with a furious honk.

"There was a fireball!" I said when I caught up with Will at the end of the level.

"Yeah. I saved your life."

"You!?"

"I told you we each get a fireball."

I shook my head.

"I think I did," said Will.

"I think I'd remember."

"Well you forgot to look out for barrels."

I huffed. There really was no point in arguing with my brother. "Is there anything else I should know?"

"How to say thank you?"

"I mean about the game," I said.

"Probably." Will shrugged. "But we'll have to find it out together. No one's ever got this far."

THE FINAL LEVEL

There are legends about what happens if you complete *Barrel Boing II*. Some claim the game blows up, others that a map appears with directions to a fortune in doubloons, while one rumour hints at a terrible curse involving relentless pecking by an angry goose. But most people just assume barrels and fish come so fast that no one ever wins.

None of that is right.

"Shouldn't something be happening?" I asked Will as we stood at the top of the ladder on the final level.

"Perhaps we won?" said Will, and he took a step forward.

The **PIRATE**, who had been standing as still as a very hairy statue, turned to us.

"Swab suds!" came a booming electronic voice. "Prepare for game ovaaaaar!"

The **PIRATE** jumped and slid across the screen until he was right above us.

"Definitely haven't won!" I yelled.

We ran under the flying **PIRATE** and towards the exit. For a second it seemed we might actually make it.

Then the **PIRATE** crashed down. The platform shook and we fell onto our boxy bottoms.

Behind us the **PIRATE** roared and jumped back towards the exit. With each jump the platform shook and with each shake Will and I bounced back to the start of the ramp.

"What was that?" I asked as we got to our feet.

"The final challenge," said Will.

The **PIRATE** flew into the

air again, faster this time. Will and I dashed forwards, the **PIRATE** landed, we fell and bounced back again.

"This is ridiculous," I said. "We can't get anywhere."

"There'll be a way," said Will. "We just have to work it out."

Up went the **PIRATE**, forward we ran, down came the **PIRATE** and back we went. Each time the pattern repeated the **PIRATE** got faster.

"It can't be impossible," said Will. "That's not the way games work."

UP, forward, DOWN, back. Over and over, faster and faster, until we barely had time to scramble away from the **PIRATE**'s leap.

"We won't survive many more jumps," said Will. "We have to try something else."

A thought came to me. "I could fireball him."

FIREBALL

In all the excitement of reaching the final level
I nearly forgot I had a fireball.

"A fireball could work," said Will. "Wait till we
run under, then shoot."

The **PIRATE** jumped, we ran for the
exit, but then I stopped and turned.

And realized I had no idea how to shoot a fireball.

I would have kicked myself with frustration,
only the game wouldn't let me do that. So I did
the only thing I could: I jumped.

The **PIRATE** crashed down. The platform
shook and Will fell over. But I landed back on my feet.

The **PIRATE** roared and leapt back to the exit.

I ran back to my brother, dodging under the
PIRATE's leaps.

"Did you see that?" I asked as Will picked himself up. "I didn't fall!"

"OK." Will looked confused.

"I didn't know how to do a fireball, so I jumped," I explained.

Will shook his head.

"It's the secret to winning the game," I said. "You have to jump when the **PIRATE** lands."

Will still looked confused.

"What?" I asked.

"Why did you come back?"

I shrugged. "To save your life. Now we're even."

The **PIRATE** cut our conversation short by launching himself back into the air.

Will and I dashed forward, but this time, just before the **PIRATE** landed, we jumped.

The **PIRATE** slammed down, the platform trembled and we landed on our feet.

"Run!" I shouted.

Behind us the **PIRATE** roared as usual, then began to leap back to the exit. We leapt each time he landed, but with each jump he gained on us.

"Run faster!" I shouted.

"Can't," said Will. "The game only has one speed."

The **PIRATE**'s next leap would bring him down right on top of us.

"You just think: 'shoot fireball'," yelled Will.

"What?"

"That's how you shoot. Just think about it."

I turned just as the **PIRATE** was about to

make his final jump. *Shoot fireball!* I thought.

Flame leapt out of my hand and smacked into the **PIRATE**. The fireball exploded with a pathetic puff of smoke that didn't so much as singe a hair on his beard.

"Flames will nae help ya," the **PIRATE** cackled.

"No," I said. "But you laughing like an idiot will."

I ran to the exit where my brother was waiting. The pixelated **PIRATE**'s laugh turned into a howl.

"Ready player one?" asked Will.

And we stepped out of the game.

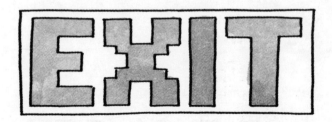

SPACE SUITS

I was back in the real world and something was wrong.

That wasn't surprising given recent experiences, but this was a new kind of wrong.

My arms were stiff – like the time it snowed and Mum made me put on five jumpers. And my eyes weren't working either; everything was fish-bowl shaped.

"Will?" I said.

"Just here," said a muffled voice from behind me.

Oh great, I thought. *My ears are broken too.*

I turned around, which took a while because I was having trouble with my legs. Will slowly came into view.

"What are you wearing?" I asked.

Will struck a ridiculous pose. "Cool isn't it? I coded space suits into the transmogrifier so we'd have them when we got out of the computer."

"Are we…?"

Will nodded. "On *McSnottbeard*'s moon."

I thought about it for a second. "Am I wearing the same thing as you?"

Will scrunched his nose and titled his head to the side in that way that people do when they mean "kind of".

"What do you mean?" I said, making the same expression.

"This is the sporty model," said Will. "I figure you are a safety-first kind of girl."

He was right, but I suspected he was most definitely wrong too. "I can't move."

"That's the padding," said Will, giving me two thumbs-up.

"I can't walk!" I shouted. The sound echoed around my helmet.

"Oh," said Will. "Not even a bit?"

I took a few unsteady steps towards Will, then toppled over and bounced.

"That's going to be a problem," said Will, rolling me onto my back and pulling me up. "Walking was how I planned to get to that." He pointed over my shoulder.

I turned around very slowly, and was suddenly grateful that I couldn't move.

MOON BASE

"Wow," I said.

"I know," said Will.

We stared for a bit longer – it was the kind of building that demanded staring.

"*McSnottbeard*'s fortress," my brother said.

We stared some more.

"Will," I said, after a while. "There's no door."

"What?"

"At the bottom," I said. "There's no opening."

Will scratched his head.

"How do we get in?" I asked.

Will scratched some more then poked my space suit. "I have a plan."

I looked at Will. I couldn't quite tell but I strongly suspected he was smiling behind his mask.

UPS AND DOWNS

I was on my back looking up at Will. He was definitely smiling now. And laughing.

I wasn't doing either – not even nearly.

I was particularly not smiling or laughing each time I hit the ground, which was happening way too often, because I was bouncing.

More precisely, I was bouncing across the moon while Will sat on me.

"It's working!" giggled Will.

Jets fired out of his boots, shooting us even higher.

"Make it stop!" I begged.

My stomach lurched as we reached the top of a particularly high bounce and headed back down again.

"*Please* make it stop!" I screamed.

"Can't," said Will. "There's so little gravity that we are going to have to bounce till we hit something."

RISKYPEDIA
The Adventurer's Encyclopedia

>> GRAVITY

Gravity is the invisible force that makes things stick to the ground. It's kind of like chewing gum you step in, but bigger and less likely to get you in trouble if you walk it into the house. Also, much like chewing gum, there isn't a lot of it on small moons in remote space.

CRASH

With each bounce we got higher.

And we were already high.

Very high.

"Will," I shouted as we rose up yet again. "Just before, when you said, 'We'll stop when we hit something'…"

"Yeah," said Will.

"It sounded a little bit like you were planning on us hitting something."

Will nodded.

"Is that a good idea?" I asked.

"Let's find out," said Will.

And we crashed through a window into *McSnottbeard*'s fortress.

CAPTURED

I landed in a shower of glass. There was a loud pop as my space suit exploded, leaving me very suddenly back in my pyjamas.

Behind me Will fired his jets, hovered briefly in the air and cried, "Ta dah!"

Then he added, "Uh … oh."

A metal hand picked me up by my pyjamas. My helmet tipped off as I swung helplessly in the air, suspended from a B.U.R.P.

The robot pointed at Will. "Halt intruder!" it droned.

"OK," said Will.

I looked at my brother. "What do you mean 'OK'?"

Will shrugged and pressed a button on his space suit. It neatly folded in on itself until it disappeared. "What else am I going to do? There's a killer robot standing in front of the door, we are hundreds of metres off the ground and we are both in our pyjamas."

"You could fight it!"

"It's made of metal!"

I hit the robot's leg with my fist. There was a dull clunk and pain shot up my arm. The robot didn't even notice.

"Ye will come with me," said the B.U.R.P. as it turned towards a door, which slid open with a hiss.

Will nodded and walked out into a corridor.

The B.U.R.P. followed and so did I.

I didn't have much choice.

THOSE MOVIES

We made our way to a sliding door that turned out to be the entrance to a lift. The B.U.R.P. pressed a button marked "**PIRATE** KING". Then it reached down and picked Will up by his pyjamas so we were hanging side by side.

"What's the plan?" I asked as the lift rose.

Will looked at me blankly. "Plan?"

"You always have a plan," I said. "You probably saw it in a movie."

Will shook his head.

"*Robot's Revenge?*" I suggested.

TINCAN TECHNO TRASHERS

Will shook his head again.

"*Tincan Techno Trashers?*"

My brother reached out and took my hand. That was a bad sign. Will never holds my hand.

"There's no plan," said Will.

"What?"

"There never were any movies."

I wasn't following. "What do you mean?"

"I made the movies up," said Will.

"Which ones?" I asked.

"All of them."

A FOOLPROOF PLAN

My jaw dropped. "WHAT?!" I yelled.

"Well, everything was weird and scary," said Will a little defensively. "I wanted to make you feel better and I thought it'd help if I seemed to know what I was doing."

I looked at my brother.

Then looked some more.

And a bit more.

"You lied?" I said.

Will shrugged. "It says on the first page that someone does."

"I didn't think it would be you!"

"I was trying to help. Anyway, it's worked so far."

The only reason my jaw didn't drop any more was because it was already at full drop.

"We are in a terrifying fortress a gazillion miles from home, hanging by our pyjamas from an evil robot that's lugging us to the universe's most horrible **PIRATE**." I slapped my free hand on the robot's thigh to emphasize each point. "How exactly has it 'worked so far'?"

Will thought for a second. "We got past the slime in our house didn't we? And captured a flying saucer. We survived the slugs and their fire lizard. We escaped a prison mine. We even beat *Barrel Boing*!"

I frowned.

"We never once really knew what we were doing," said Will.

My frown deepened.

"And we still don't," he added with a hopeful smile.

I shook my head in disbelief. "So having no plan – that's our plan?"

My brother's smile faded. He looked at the ground then back at me.

He was scared.

In fact he was probably just about as scared as I had been when I discovered the slime in our house, and when we arrived on the mother ship, and when the dragon was trying to grill us, and … basically every time Will had invented a film to make me feel better.

I found myself wanting to make him feel better. So, I did the only thing I could.

"No plan sounds like a great plan," I lied as I squeezed his hand. "At least it can't go wrong."

The lift stopped with a cheerful *bing*. "Level **PIRATE** king," came a voice from a speaker. "*McSnottbeard*, killer robots and the big finale. Please watch your step."

Then the doors slid open and I was suddenly glad we had no plan.

Nothing we could have come up with would have worked.

BARMY ARMY

We stepped out of the lift – or at least the robot did.

Outside the door was an improbably large hangar, four storeys high and as big as two football pitches. But that wasn't the reason any plan would have failed.

On the far side of the hangar a massive
PIRATE galleon floated in front of a wide
opening into space. But that wasn't the
reason either.

Covering the entire floor of the hangar
were thousands of B.U.R.P.s.

That!

That was the reason!

"Cripes," said Will.

"Cripes," I said, because when faced with an
evil robot army originality isn't important.

BE CAREFUL WHAT
YOU WISH FOR

You're probably not surprised to learn that
coming face-to-face with thousands of
merciless killing machines is scary.

And it wasn't just that any one of them
could have killed us with its little toe – if they
had toes. There was also the fact that they all
vaguely resembled *McSnottbeard*, and that
every one of them watched us as we were
carried to the galleon, their heads turning in
unison as we passed.

But the spookiest thing of all was the
silence. We were in a crowd of thousands
but, apart from the clacking of our B.U.R.P.
walking, it was so quiet you could have heard

a mouse's whisker drop onto a cloud.

"I wish someone would make a noise," I
whispered to Will.

I immediately regretted it.

From the **PIRATE** galleon came the hum
of a harmonica finding a note. And then the
sound of *McSnottbeard* completely ignoring
whatever note had just been found:

*"I've an army, yes an army,
made of wires and circuits and screws.
With my army, massive army,
there's no way that I can lose.
We are heading to Earth,
probably crush Europe first,*

*Then the US and all the rest!
No plan is too barmy cause
my robot army's the best.*

I've got robots, lots of robots, and they
do whatever I say.
  With my robots, deadly robots,
everybody is going to pay.
  They are better than goons
at collecting doubloons,
    I'll be rich beyond all my dreams!
    I'll have lots and lots, cause as well as
robots they are thieves.

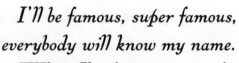

    I'll be famous, super famous,
everybody will know my name.
  When I'm famous, mega famous,
no more sniggering at my shame.
    In government halls and on all the
school walls,
    There'll be photos and paintings of me!
    I'll sing in Las Vegas, that's how super
famous I'll be."

The song finished (thankfully) just as we arrived at the bottom of a gangplank that led onto the galleon.

Above us perched on the railing was *McSnottbeard*. "Arrrrrr," said the **PIRATE**, because that's how **PIRATES** start almost every sentence. "If it isn't the wee crab scabs. Just in time."

"For what?"

I really shouldn't have asked.

"TO DIE!" roared *McSnottbeard*.

EVEN THE PIRATE HAS A PLAN!

We were carried onto the deck of the ship and dropped in front of *McSnottbeard*, who was now sitting in a deep leather chair – the kind that all super villains seem to own.

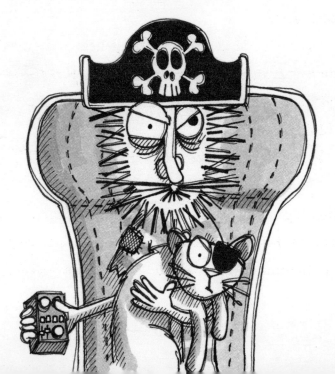

A line of B.U.R.P.s stood still (and menacingly) behind the **PIRATE**.

In one hand he had a small black box, while his other held a miserable-looking cat with an eyepatch.

"Eiffel!" I said as I picked myself up from the deck. "What happened to your eye?"

"Nothing," huffed the cat. "He makes me wear it."

"And your fur?"

"I'm not allowed to wash. Apparently it's a **PIRATE** thing."

McSnottbeard chuckled and stroked Eiffel's fur backwards.

My cat made the sort of face I generally reserve for beans, then struggled out of the **PIRATE**'s grasp and climbed up to a cross beam on the ship's mast.

Will stood and stepped towards the **PIRATE**.

"That's close enough," said *McSnottbeard*, flicking the little black box with his finger. The B.U.R.P.s stepped forward to form a terrifying mechanical wall between us and *McSnottbeard*.

"Nifty ain't they?" said *McSnottbeard*. "Does whatever I tells 'em."

I must have looked confused.

"What?" the **PIRATE** growled.

"It's just…" I hesitated. "Why didn't you use the robots to kidnap our parents? Why go through all that bother with the slugs?"

"Number one on your list of things worth knowing about **PIRATES**," said *McSnottbeard*. "**PIRATE** plans don't have to make sense as long as they are nasty."

"You've read my lists?" I smiled. I was happy to have found a fan – even a horrible one.

Will clearly didn't care about the life of a writer.

"What did you do with our parents?" he said, changing the subject.

"Is that why you're 'ere?" the **PIRATE** sneered. "For those old salt sacks?"

"They are our family," said Will.

"No," said *McSnottbeard*. "They were ye family."

I gasped. "You killed them?"

GULLS AND BUOYS

McSnottbeard laughed.

"Killed ye parents?" he said. "I like how ye think. But nae. I'm using them."

"For what?" I asked.

"Signs," said *McSnottbeard*. "I've hung ye mother outside the ladies' loo and your dad outside the gents'. That way me visitors will know which toilet to use."

"Visitors?" Will asked.

GULLS   BUOYS

"Aye, me robot army is nearly ready for action, and once the world gets a gander at 'em I'll have every leader coming onboard begging me to spare their pathetic country."

I was stunned. "You're using our parents for toilet signs? That's awful!"

"Thanks." *McSnottbeard* grinned.

"It won't work," said Will.

"Sure it will," said the **PIRATE**. "Couldn't be easier: a woman for the women's toilet and a—"

"I mean invading Earth."

McSnottbeard shrugged. "I've got a few thousand reasons to think it will."

The **PIRATE** pressed a button on the little black box. Down in the hangar the B.U.R.P.s snapped to attention with a thunderous clunk of their feet and raised their swords in perfect unison.

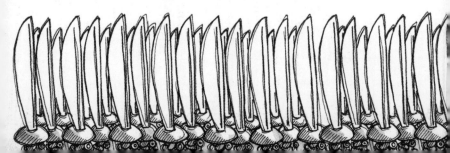

Here are my four strategies for surviving an invasion by a robot army:

Things Worth Knowing No. 11
by Emilie

1) Hide and hope their batteries go flat.

2) Pray for rain and wait for rust.

3) Draw a face on a box. Put the box on your head. Try to blend in.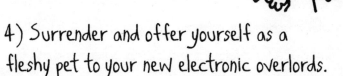

4) Surrender and offer yourself as a fleshy pet to your new electronic overlords.

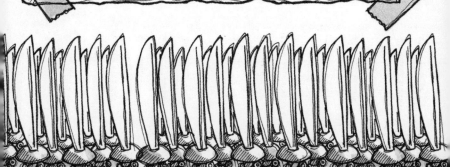

I grabbed hold of Will's pyjamas, partly out of fright, but also to pull him closer. I pointed at the little black box.

"That thingamy in his hand – it controls the robots. If we can get it, then *we* can control the robots," I said.

My brother nodded. "When I say go," he whispered out the corner of his mouth, "you do something to distract him and I'll grab it."

And just like that, we had a plan.

A (VERY LITTLE) BIT OF MAGIC

Will stepped forwards, stopping just out of reach of the B.U.R.P.s' swords "This ends now!" he shouted.

"This should be good." The **PIRATE** leaned back in his chair. "Tell me how?"

"You surrender and hand over our parents," Will said confidently. "Or I magic up an army that'll rip your tin-can soldiers into foil strips."

That isn't as weird as it sounds. My brother conjured an army the last time we fought *McSnottbeard*. There were dinosaurs, zombies and even a werewolf. *McSnottbeard* got so scared he ran off.

Only, this time, he didn't look scared. "Arrrrr.
Go smoke a kipper ye snivelling sand sprat,"
he chuckled. "I knows as well as ye do that
in space ye can't so much as conjure a puff of
smoke."

Will's eyes narrowed into a determined stare.
He raised his arms in that way that wizards do
when they are about to cast a spell. "You are
wrong," he said.

"Prove it," growled *McSnottbeard*.

Will brought his hands together in a
thunderous clap.

Nothing happened.

"Pufffff," said my brother and waggled his
fingers in a rough estimation of smoke.

McSnottbeard burst out laughing.

"Go, Emilie!" shouted Will, and he lunged for
a gap in the wall of B.U.R.P.s.

I started to dance.

ONE LAST THING

In the next moment I learned two things about B.U.R.P.s.

The first is that they don't get distracted. The second is that their hands make a curiously hollow yet solid noise when they hit a human head. If you had to describe it you might say it was a smack mixed with a clunk.

Or kind of a

Will collapsed to the ground, clutching his head.

"Pathetic." *McSnottbeard* tutted. The **PIRATE** turned his gaze to me. "What in the seven seas are you doing?"

I stopped dancing and lowered my arms. "Boogaloo Chicken," I mumbled.

"It's awful!"

I nodded.

"Don't do it again."

"OK," I said. "Are you going to kill me now?"

"My wee prawn fart," growled *McSnottbeard*, "killing you is the last thing I want to do."

That was a surprise.

"OK," I said. "Thanks."

"What? No!" The **PIRATE** looked confused. "I am going to kill you. Just last."

SLOW, STEADY AND DEADLY

McSnottbeard sat back in his chair. "Actually," he said, "come to think of it, I am not going to kill either of you."

"Oh," I said. "Thanks."

"I am going to let them do it." He motioned to the B.U.R.P.s.

I made a mental note to stop thanking the **PIRATE**.

McSnottbeard tapped the controller. The robots on the boat sprang to life. They raised their swords and marched towards my brother, forming a tight circle around him as he sat rubbing his head.

"How should we do this?" the **PIRATE**

pondered as he rubbed his chin. "I think …
slow."

McSnottbeard twisted a dial on the black
box. The robots turned their sword points
down and began to lower them, slowly.

Will tried to squirm through the B.U.R.P. legs
but the gap was too narrow.

"I can't get out!" he yelled.

"Well I'm not coming in," I said.

"Get the controller!"

I spun to face *McSnottbeard*. He was still
reclining in his chair, only now he was pointing
a large musket at me.

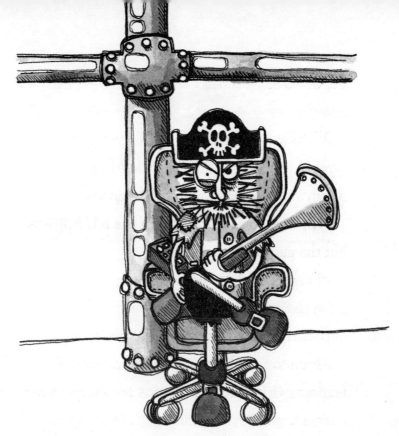

"My promise to kill you last is flexible," said the **PIRATE**.

"Hurry," shouted Will.

"He's got a very big gun," I said.

"I have a few very small seconds!" replied Will.

I took an uncertain step towards *McSnottbeard*. The **PIRATE** shook his head. "Aaaaay couldn't possibly miss from this close."

HELP FROM
ON HIGH

Something small, white and no longer wearing an eyepatch flashed along the mast then plummeted with an ear-piercing wail.

McSnottbeard let out a scream as our cat landed on his head and dug in his claws. A blast roared from the gun. Pellets flew over my head and pinged harmlessly off the back of a B.U.R.P.

"Eiffel?" I said.

"Get the controller!" Eiffel
shouted as he raked
his claws across the
PIRATE's eye.

IP, DIP, SKY BLUE

I ducked a flailing **PIRATE** leg and snatched the controller off the armrest.

"Got it!" I yelled. "I got the … thingamy."

"Great!" shouted my brother, who was now lying as flat as he could on his back. "Stop the swords!"

I looked down at the little black box. There were buttons and dials all over it.

"How?"

"The off button!"

"Which one's that?"

"I don't know!" yelled Will.

"Neither do I," I replied. "If I did I wouldn't be calling this a thingamy."

"I am running out of time, Emilie!"

I twirled a knob. The B.U.R.P.s' swords accelerated.

"Not that one!" screamed Will.

I twisted the knob back. The swords slowed just an inch from skewering my brother.

I chose three off-ish looking buttons. "Ip, dip, sky blue, who's it, not you…"

"We don't have time for that!" cried Will. The tips of the swords were pressing down on the folds of my brother's pyjamas. Will turned his head to the side as one of them touched his cheek.

I jabbed my finger down hard on the controller.

Too hard.

The box toppled out of my hand and turned over and over in that slow-motion way that all tragedies happen, then hit the floor.

Springs and dials skittered across the ground.

"Ooops!" I said.

RUN! (AGAIN)

I clapped my hands over my ears to block out Will's screams. It didn't work. No matter how hard I pressed I could still hear howling.

And laughing.

Which was strange. People don't usually do both at once.

I unblocked an ear.

"AAAAARRRRRGH!" came the scream, but not from Will. It was *McSnottbeard* who was still battling to get the cat off his face.

"Haha!" laughed my brother from under the B.U.R.P.s' motionless swords. "You found the button!"

I picked up some of the shattered controller. "Sure," I said.

Behind me the **PIRATE** roared and something furry sailed over my head with a yowl. I looked up to see Eiffel land on the deck of the boat.

McSnottbeard rose from his chair. He was bleeding from a scratch that ran up his cheek and over an eye that had swollen shut.

"I am going to kill you first after all," he snarled as he threw the empty musket to the ground and drew a sword and a knife.

"Run!" shouted Eiffel.

THAT ONE
BIG
THING

I scrambled across the deck after the cat.
He stopped briefly to make sure I was following
then disappeared down some stairs into the ship.

I leapt down the steps two at a time and
landed in a narrow corridor. Up ahead the cat
was pacing nervously in front of a closed door.

"Are you on our side now?" I asked when
I caught up.

Eiffel shot me an injured look. "I was always
on your side."

"But back on the mother ship you said…"

"I was lying," said the cat. "I had to stay next

to *McSnottbeard* if I was going to keep an eye on your parents."

"But—"

"Don't be so surprised," said Eiffel. "It says on the first page there's a big lie in this book."

"Nice try," I said. "Will used that already."

"What?" said Eiffel. "No. That, on the first page, is the lie."

I gave the cat a confused look.

"William lied to you," explained the cat. "*McSnottbeard* lied to the slugs, I lied to everyone. Even you lied to Will. The big lie is that there's only one big lie in this book."

I nodded, but even as I did something else occurred to me. If the truth was that there was more than one lie, then the cat could still be lying. Which meant…

My thoughts were interrupted by some very bad and uncomfortably close singing.

"Ye cannae hide from me,
I'll find you soon you'll see.
This sea dog's snout
Will sniff you out,
Then I'll cut you up with glee.

Every nook will be explored
And poked with this here sword,
Cause I knows this ship
From its stern to its tip,
And from port to its
starboard."

I heard footsteps at the top of the stairs.
"Ready or not here I come," growled
McSnottbeard.

ESCAPE POD

I shoved open the door. Eiffel shot ahead of me
and led the way through a maze of corridors
and down a spiral staircase deeper into the ship.
"Where are we going?" I puffed as we descended.

"The escape pods," said Eiffel.

"Woah!" I stopped and held up my hand.
"Before we go any further you have to answer
some questions."

"Really?" The cat looked nervously back up
the stairs.

I nodded and held up a finger.

"FIRST," I said. "How do you know there are escape pods?"

I flicked up another finger. "SECOND. How do you know where they are?"

"THIRD. Do you know how they work?"

"FOURTH. Are they big enough for four people?"

"Because, FIFTH," I said, flicking out my thumb. "Do you really think I would leave without my brother and my parents?"

"We don't have time for this," said Eiffel.

I crossed my arms and planted my feet. I wasn't moving until I got answers.

"Fine. I don't have fingers so you will just have to keep up," said the cat. "FIRST, I've been the only living thing *McSnottbeard* has had to talk to and he never shuts up about this boat. SECOND, I've been trying to avoid him, so I know all the out of the way spots. THIRD, cats come from a planet that was destroyed by alien slug monsters – we know a thing or two about escape pods. FOURTH, we can't all fit. And FIFTH, that isn't going to be a problem."

There was a creak up above us. A horrible, bristly face leered over the railing. "Lickety-split, I'm it!" yelled *McSnottbeard*.

I jumped about a foot in the air. Eiffel was already at the bottom of the stairs by the time I landed.

TRAPPED AND BETRAYED

I raced to keep up with Eiffel and ahead of the sound of the **PIRATE** clomping after me. The cat disappeared around a bend, then we twisted and turned through corridors until we hit a...

"Dead end," said Eiffel.

"Don't say dead," I pleaded.

In front of us was what looked very much like the top of a massive tin can, only with a round window and a wheel. Next to the can lid was a big red button with LAUNCH written underneath it.

"Is that...?" I asked.

"The escape pod," said Eiffel, who then rather confusingly sat down and started cleaning himself.

"Umm ... shouldn't you open it?" I asked.

"No hands," said the cat.

"Good point," I said and twisted the wheel.

The door swung open. Inside were two large swivel chairs facing computer screens and a thick window that offered a blurred view out to space.

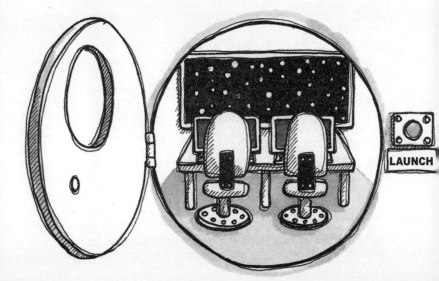

"Now what?" I asked.

"Get behind the door."

"Why? Where are you going?"

"I'm getting in."

"I knew it!" I shouted at the cat. "You lied again. The only reason you brought me here was because you couldn't open the escape pod. Oh, you are a bad, bad cat and I am never, ever, changing your litter tray again."

"You never did," said the cat.

"Fee fi fo faaaar!" came a gravelly voice from not far enough away. "I'll get ye wherever y'aaar."

There was no way out that didn't lead back to the **PIRATE**. Our only hope was that *McSnottbeard* wouldn't find us. It was a slim hope, but perhaps if we stayed really, really quiet…

"We're down here!" yelled Eiffel.

PEEK-A-BOO

The cat leapt into the escape pod, climbed onto a seat and began tapping buttons on the control panel.

Behind us came the stomp of *McSnottbeard*'s boots as he approached.

"I am getting a dog," I hissed at the cat.

Eiffel's head poked around the edge of the seat. "Fine," he said. "But can I suggest that you decide on the breed from a hiding place?"

I stepped behind the outside of the escape pod's door, grabbed the metal wheel and lifted myself up so I could peek through the window.

"Ready or not here I come," growled the **PIRATE** as he rounded the corner. "Where could ye be?" he added with a wicked chuckle.

"In here," said Eiffel from the escape pod.

Through the glass I saw the **PIRATE** raise his sword at the pod's entrance. I ducked down and held tight to the wheel.

"Think ye are leaving do ye?" said *McSnottbeard*.

"Just finished programming the escape route," replied Eiffel.

A filthy hand holding a long dagger wrapped around the pod's door, just inches from my face.

I held my breath.

"I'll see you two dead before I let you leave!" rumbled the **PIRATE**.

Two? I thought. Then it dawned on me: *McSnottbeard* thought we were both in the pod.

IN THE CAN

I eased myself down to the floor and edged around the door. *McSnottbeard* stood at the escape pod entrance with his back to me.

I took a slow, quiet step away from him. And then another. And another.

I started to run.

Then I stopped.

"People can choose what kind of people they want to be," I whispered to myself. "And I choose to be the kind of person who defeats **PIRATES** and saves people. Even if the people are cats."

I took a deep breath, turned to *McSnottbeard*, and threw myself into his back.

The **PIRATE** crashed into the escape pod

with a clatter, which was quickly followed by the scream of a terrified cat.

Eiffel shot out of the pod's door, twisted in mid-air and stopped with a skittering of claws on the floor.

"SHUT IT!" screamed the cat.

"Well that's rude."

"THE DOOR!"

"Oh."

I grabbed the escape pod's hatch and peered inside. *McSnottbeard* looked out at me from barely a metre away, his one good eye bloodshot with rage, his sword pointed directly at my neck.

"Time to die ye mangy mullet!" The **PIRATE** lunged at me.

A smile flicked across my face.

"Not today ye putrid **PIRATE**."

I slammed the door shut and spun the wheel. There was the satisfying click of a lock fastening and then the even more satisfying thud of a **PIRATE** slamming into solid metal.

LAUNCH

I looked at the button marked LAUNCH then down at Eiffel.

"Shall I?" I asked.

"It's not like I can reach it," said the cat.

I whacked my hand against the red disc.

There was a hiss and the escape pod drifted away, spinning gently so the capsule's window came into view. *McSnottbeard*'s face was pressed against the glass. He looked ... not quite scared, but certainly worried.

I waved. And just as I did, rockets on either
side of the pod fired.

The shuttle zoomed into space.

I picked Eiffel up and together we watched
the pod get smaller and smaller until
it looked like one of the
millions of stars.

"Where's he going?" I asked.

"To a reunion with some old friends," said Eiffel. "Slimy ones that may not be too happy to see him."

I gently scratched the back of Eiffel's ear.

"I should have trusted you," I said.

"Yeah," said Eiffel. "You should have."

"But I'm still not changing your litter tray."

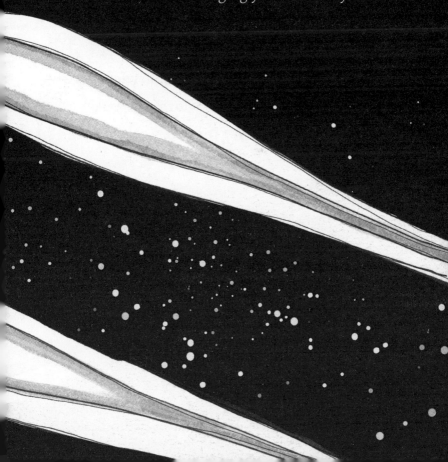

EPILOGUE

And that was that.

I mean, I could tell you about walking back up on deck (nothing happened) and freeing Will (he was lying very still under the B.U.R.P.s' swords). We found our parents (they really were hanging outside the loos, which was handy because I was bursting for a wee). We fixed the robot controller and, following a nearly-lethal false start, got the robots to cut Mum and Dad from the slime blocks.

After that there was a fair bit of hugging and quite a bit of purring.

Getting home was easy enough. *McSnottbeard* had already programmed the ship to go to Earth in preparation for his invasion.

Landing a spaceship in our backyard caused a bit of a stir (you might have read about it in the papers). But people's attention moves on quickly enough and before we knew it we were back to being just an ordinary family – albeit one that has killer robots to help around the house.

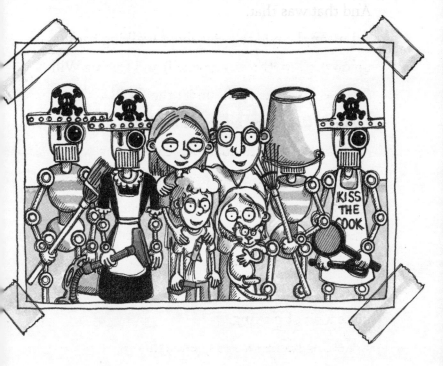

And ordinary was just how things remained.

Unless you count the time our parents were kidnapped by a horde of time-travelling Viking beserkers...

THE END

ABOUT THE AUTHOR

Paul Whitfield was born in Australia, and has,
mostly by accident, been a business journalist since 1997.
He has written for Bloomberg, the BBC, the New York
Times and several British national newspapers.
Pirate McSnottbeard in the Alien Slug Invasion Panic
is the second book in his Pirate McSnottbeard series.

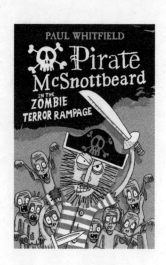